Anna Kavan

Anna Kavan, née Helen Woods, was born in Cannes – probably in 1901; she was evasive about the facts of her life– and spent her childhood in Europe, the United States and Great Britain. Her life was haunted by her rich, glamorous mother, beside whom her father remains an indistinct figure. Twice married and divorced, she began writing while living with her first husband in Burma and was at first published under her married name of ,Helen Ferguson. Her early writing consisted of somewhat eccentric 'Home Counties' novels, but her work changed after her second marriage collapsed. In the wake of this, she suffered the first of many nervous breakdowns and was confined to a clinic in Switzerland. She emerged from her incarceration with a new name – Anna Kavan, the protagonist of her 1930 novel *Let Me Alone* – an outwardly different persona and a new literary style. She suffered periodic bouts of mental illness and long-term drug addiction – she became dependent on heroin in the 1920s and continued to use it throughout her life – and these facets of her biography feature prominently in her work. She destroyed almost all her personal correspondence and most of her diaries, therefore ensuring that she achieved her ambition to become 'one of the world's best-kept secrets'. She died in 1968 of heart failure soon after the publication of her most celebrated work, the novel *Ice*.

By the same author
Asylum Piece
A Bright Green Field (stories)
Change the Name
A Charmed Circle
Eagle's Nest
Guilty
I Am Lazarus (stories)
Ice
Let Me Alone
Mercury
My Soul in China (novella and stories)
The Parson
A Scarcity of Love
Sleep Has His House
A Stranger Still
Who Are You?

JULIA AND THE BAZOOKA

ANNA KAVAN

JULIA AND THE BAZOOKA

With a foreword by Virginia Ironside

PETER OWEN
London and Chester Springs, PA, USA

PETER OWEN PUBLISHERS
73 Kenway Road, London SW5 0RE

Peter Owen books are distributed in the USA by Dufour Editions Inc.,
Chester Springs, PA 19425–0007

First published by Peter Owen 1970
© Rhys Davies and R.B. Marriott 1970, 2009
This Peter Owen Modern Classics edition 2009
Introduction © Virginia Ironside 2009

ISBN 978-0-7206-1328-5

A catalogue record for this book is available
from the British Library

Printed by CPI Bookmarque, Croydon, CR0 4TD

Introduction

In the late 1950s I used to play tennis at courts just off Church Street in London's Notting Hill Gate. None of us were any good, and I would always return home with a gloomy headache, which used to be cured, oddly, with a refreshing spoonful of vinegar.

Older, I hoped to have put those dreadful hot days behind me, until a few years ago I became obsessed with the work of an almost unknown writer, the late Anna Kavan. The book that started me off on my Kavan obsession was this one, *Julia and the Bazooka*, and after that I devoured all of her books in one fell swoop.

She wrote of lunatic asylums, feelings of alienation, addiction – her internal loneliness was tangible. Desperate for more information about this fascinating woman who seemed to be describing a place of suffering I knew well, I discovered that not only had she spent the last half of her life in Notting Hill, just down the road from where I used to play tennis, but that she described, in a letter to a friend of hers, the sound of the balls on Campden Tennis Courts. Had I perhaps bumped into her as I stomped back home?

And who was she, this enigmatic, doomed creature who, it turned out, in a 1964 survey, was one of the 753 heroin addicts recorded in England at the time?

Born Helen Woods, she then became Helen Ferguson and

later Helen Edmonds but, quite early in her life, destroyed all her diaries and papers, adopted a new birth date, a new physical appearance, a new persona, a new literary style and a new name – Anna Kavan. 'I was about to become the world's best-kept secret, one that would never be told. What a thrilling enigma for posterity I should be,' she wrote.

Unfortunately for us, she's been a bit too much of a secret, despite being discovered again and again over the years. For instance, Jonathan Cape published *Asylum Piece*, her first book written as Anna Kavan in 1940. 'At last I did produce something really good, something quite out of the ordinary, if I say it myself,' she wrote. 'The preliminary reviews were first rate, everything seemed set for success. You've really brought it off this time, Jonathan said. Then the war started. That was the end of that.'

Cyril Connolly would not have asked her to work for him at *Horizon*, the literary magazine, had he not admired her work, Anaïs Nin described her as 'an equal to Kafka', Doris Lessing rediscovered her, then J.G. Ballard and Brian Aldiss declared her to be a truly great science-fiction writer. Even the *New Yorker* raved over one of her books. She was 'a writer of such chillingly matter-of-fact, unself-pitying vigour that her vision transcends itself', wrote the reviewer.

It's to be hoped that the republication of this splendid book will enable Anna Kavan to be rediscovered yet again; this time, perhaps, for good.

True, she's not a writer for those who like uplifting books or happy endings. She writes of a terrifying inner landscape of evil and threat – a landscape that she seemed to inhabit for most of her life. All is arid and destitute, every minute is spent waiting for a reprieve that never comes or, worse, a punishment. 'To whom can one appear when one does not even know where to find the judge? How can one ever hope to find one's innocence when there is no means of knowing of what one has been accused?' she wrote in one story.

And yet, for anyone who has experienced the merest whisper of true depression or mental illness, her books – with titles such as *Let Me Alone*, *A Scarcity of Love*, *I Am Lazarus* – are strangely reassuring and comforting. Reading them is like coming across a guide to a country you thought that only you had visited. She writes of it with fear, with respect, with elegance, with art and style – and often with black humour. But she writes as a true citizen of that strange interface between reality and hell.

She was born Helen Woods in Cannes in 1901. Her mother, with whom she had an extremely difficult relationship, was an avid socialite who frequently abandoned her strange only child – first to a wet-nurse, then nannies, nurses, an aunt and finally to boarding-schools in America, France and eventually Malvern Girls' College, which she hated. (When at school, she later wrote, 'One day when I combed my hair in front of the mirror, my mother looked out at me with her face of an exiled princess. That was the day I knew I was unhappy.')

When she was fourteen her father jumped overboard to his death from a liner bound for South America, and Anna's mother was left badly off. Although, at nineteen, Anna begged to be allowed to go to Oxford, her mother refused and encouraged her to marry one of her own cast-off lovers, Donald Ferguson, an engineer on the Burmese Railways. They set off for Mandalay, via Rangoon, and to pass the time and relieve the stress of a miserable liaison she started writing.

After a while, Anna left her young son with her increasingly boorish husband and got divorced. It was then that she fell into the company of racing drivers in the South of France, which she describes in the story 'World of Heroes'. 'At last I belonged somewhere, had a place, was some use in the world. For the very first time I understood the meaning of happiness, and it was easy for me to be truly in love with each of them . . . Out of their great generosity, they gave me the truth, paid me the compliment of not lying to me. Not one of them ever told me life was worth living. They are the only people I've ever loved.'

And it was the racing drivers who introduced her to what was to become a life-long addiction to heroin. She didn't need much encouragement. She was already using cocaine, having been recommended it by a tennis coach in the South of France 'to improve her serve'.

Heroin was her friend. In 'High in the Mountains' she writes, 'What I do never affects anyone else. I don't behave in an embarrassing way. And a clean white powder is not repulsive; it looks pure, it glitters, the pure white crystals sparkle like snow.'

Six of the stories here, including, of course, the title story, 'Julia and the Bazooka' (she referred to her syringe as her 'bazooka') refer in some way to her addiction. And, apart, perhaps, from Stefan Zweig's *Twenty-four Hours in the Life of a Woman* I have never read anything so utterly poignant and frighteningly honest as 'The Old Address', in which she describes the grim and lonely process of leaving rehab and . . . but you'll have to find out yourself.

Her next relationship – no one is certain whether she actually married him or not – was to an alcoholic artist called Stuart Edmonds, and her life with him in rural Buckinghamshire is agonizingly described in 'Now and Then'. Anyone who has been involved with an addict of any kind will recognize the Jekyll-and-Hyde characteristics that sour such a relationship.

Eventually, in the early 1950s she left him and settled in Notting Hill Gate. She spotted that was an up-and-coming area and formed, with an architect friend, Kavan Properties, the object of which was to buy, refurbish and sell houses. This made – with a small allowance – enough to live as a writer.

Her garden – written about so beautifully in 'A Town Garden' – was apparently like a painting by Rousseau, densely foliated with fig trees, rhododendrons, wistaria, tall grasses and laurels and guarded by such high walls (built by Anna) that the neighbours complained.

Every day she wrote for three hours – and every afternoon she would head out to buy books or go up to Soho to buy her favourite *mille feuilles*. And Anna was not, of course, the kind of heroin addict you think of these days. She was genteel, properly brought up and never 'let herself go' – always dressed immaculately, her platinum hair beautifully set. Even in summer she would often wear a fur coat, being, as addicts so often are, permanently cold. Apparently she had a quiet husky voice and spoke in slow affected drawl like Marlene Dietrich and Jean Harlow

Heroin was easily available on the black market in London. Members of fashionable society bought their supplies from a Chinaman, Mr 'Brilliant' Chang or Lady Frankau, a GP who prescribed heroin to her patients. But Anna had another person to rely on as her dealer – Dr Theodor Bluth, a married psychiatrist who lived around the corner from her in Campden Street. It was with Dr Bluth that she had her most intense – though platonic – relationship. It was Dr Bluth who persuaded her to register with the Home Office as a heroin addict so that he could supply her, legally, until his death.

Dr Bluth, much older than Anna, was a maverick psychiatrist who had escaped from Germany before the war. wrote poetry and hammered away on a white piano in his Notting Hill surgery before he injected his patients with mixture of ox blood and methadone. Sometimes his weary patients came away from Campden Street pumped full of amphetamines and B vitamins.

Kavan met Dr Bluth on one of her many detoxes – but her heart was never in getting off heroin. She saw it as a normalizing, cathartic experience, not one to give you a great high – and she was using heroin in this way long before people such as Keith Richards, William Burroughs, Alan Ginsberg and Aldous

Huxley had ever heard of the stuff.

She was obsessed with Bluth and appeared to live for his spasmodic visits – and not just because of his welcome doses of heroin. Three of the stories in this books are clearly about Bluth, 'Mercedes', 'The Zebra Struck' and 'Obsessional', in which she wrote, 'She did not wish to escape the consciousness of him, which nevertheless was a burden, like a dead body she carried about everywhere and couldn't bear to relinquish.' When he departs he leaves her 'with a famished longing so acute that is seemed physical and hardly to be endured'.

When Dr Bluth died she became suicidal, and, rescued from a suicide attempt by friends, she complained, 'I can't say how profoundly I resent their interference.' She had never enjoyed life and in 1926 had written, 'Real life is a hateful and tiresome dream.' In 1965 life was 'just a nightmare and the universe has no meaning'.

Dr Bluth's death not only caused Anna intense grief but a huge drug problem. In 1961 an interdepartmental committee called the Brain Committee recommended that heroin addicts should attend out-patient clinics to get their fixes. Terrified that she might be forced to undergo compulsory detoxification, she frantically stockpiled supplies in her bathroom.

She died of a heart attack in the winter of 1968, on the evening she was due to attend a Notting Hill party given by her publisher, Peter Owen, to meet her greatest admirer, Anaïs Nin. She was found lying on her bed, her head on the Chinese box in which she kept her drugs. Later, the police said they found in her house enough heroin to 'kill the whole street'.

Contents

1	The Old Address	13
2	A Visit	19
3	Fog	28
4	Experimental	37
5	World of Heroes	49
6	The Mercedes	59
7	Clarita	66
8	Out and Away	76
9	Now and Then	84
10	High in the Mountains	99
11	Among the Lost Things	107
12	The Zebra-Struck	114
13	A Town Garden	136
14	Obsessional	142
15	Julia and the Bazooka	150

The Old Address

The day Sister comes in while I'm packing to leave. She's about ten feet tall, and, as if to disguise the fact, usually adopts a slouch and keeps her hands in her pockets under the starched apron. Now, however, she has a big envelope marked Patient's Property in one hand, which she holds out to me.

'You won't need this, but we have to return it to you now you're being discharged.'

I take it. How very odd. I get a sensation like dreaming as I feel through the paper the familiar barrel-shape of the syringe I haven't felt for so long.

'It's no use anyhow,' I say to her, 'without something to put in it.' This doesn't sound quite the right thing, so I add, 'I may as well leave it here,' and drop it nonchalantly into the waste-paper basket.

She stares at me so hard that I wonder what's in her mind. Finally she shrugs her shoulders and slouches out, omitting to say goodbye.

I wait until I'm sure she's not coming back, then retrieve the envelope and put it into my bag. I've no particular object in doing so; the action seems pretty well automatic. I sit down to wait for someone to come and fetch me, but I'm too restless to keep still, so I put my coat on and walk

13

out of the ward and along a passage, past a number of people, none of whom takes the slightest notice of me.

Besides the syringe, the usual collection of things, including money, is in my bag. If anybody asks questions, I'm on my way to buy farewell presents for the nurses. Commendable, surely?

No questions are asked. The porter shoves the revolving door, I go down the steps of the main entrance and on to the pavement.

I'm outside again. Free. Also, of course, I'm still guilty, and always shall be. I don't feel anything much though, except that it's strange to be out here on my own. After a few steps strange equates with disturbing. This isn't the world I know. I look all round, at the crowds, the skyscrapers, the mass of traffic. It all looks delirious, ominous, mad.

There's an absolute mob surging along the pavement, you can't move without bumping into someone. I search in vain for a human face. Only hordes of masks, dummies, zombies go charging past, blindly, heads down. Stern condemnatory faces of magistrates glare at me from their pedestals at street corners. Cold enemy eyes, arrow-eyes, pierce me with poison-tipped suspicion, as if they know where I've come from.

Terrible eyes. Terrible noise. Terrible traffic.

The sky is full of unnatural light, which is really a darkish murk and makes everything look sinister, a black conspiracy hanging up there in the air. Something frightful seems to be happening, or going to happen.

The traffic roars, bellows, hurls itself in a torrential surge as into battle—cars thresh about like primeval monsters. Some have grins of diabolical joy on their malevolent rudimentary faces, gloating over prospective victims.

They're anticipating the moment when their murderous deadweight of hard heavy metal will tear into soft, vulnerable, defenceless flesh, mashing it into a pulp, which, thinly spread on the roadway, creates a treacherous slippery surface where other cars skid in circles, their wheels entangled in sausage-strings of entrails bursting out of the mess.

Suddenly I notice that one car has selected me as its prey and is making straight for me through all the chaos. Come on, then! Knock me down, run over me, cut off my existence. I don't want it—don't like it. I never did. The size of a locomotive, the hideous great mechanical dinosaur bears down upon me. Already the metal assassin towers over my head.

And now the dingy mass hits me with the full force of its horrid inhuman horsepower, a ton or so of old iron to finish me off. I'm demolished, done for, down on the pavement which is already black with my blood. Lying there, mangled, splintered, a smashed matchbox, all at once I find I'm transformed into an inexhaustible fountain, spouting blood like a whale.

Huge black clots, gouts, of whale-blood shoot high in the air, then splash down in the mounting flood, soaking the nearest pedestrians. Everybody is slipping and slithering, wading in blood. It's over their ankles. Now it's up to their knees. All along the street, children start screaming, licking blood off their chins, tasting it on their tongues just before they drown.

The grown-ups can't save them, they're drowning too. Fine! Splendid! Let them all drown, the bastards; they've all done their best to destroy me. I hate them all. There's no end to my blood supply. It's been turned on full at the main, at high pressure, nobody knows how to turn it off

Everywhere people are coughing and choking, their lungs are filling with my unbreathable blood, and it's poison, a deadly poison, to them.

Wonderful! At last I'm being revenged on those who have persecuted me all my life. I've always loathed the horrible hostile creatures pressing round me in a suffocating mass, trying to get me down, to trample on me. Down with them now! Now it's their turn to suffocate. I laugh in their faces, smeared and streaked like Red Indians with my blood. And all the time my broken thorax goes on pouring out blood.

They're out of their depth now. They try to swim. But their clothes are too heavy, already saturated by the thick, sticky, steaming tide. Inevitably, they are dragged under, writhing, shouting and struggling. Wasting their strength in idiotic contortions, they're all sinking and drowning already. I lash out wildly at the few survivors, hit them as hard as I can, bash them on the head, forcing them down into the sea of blood as if they were so many eels. Down, wantons, down!

Suddenly the show's over. Sudden lightning strikes overhead. A forked tree of blinding brilliance flares up the sky, setting fire to it as it goes. In a flash, the whole sky is a sheet of flame, consumed, gone up in smoke. Nothing is left where the sky used to be except an expanse of grimy canvas, like the walls of a tent. No wonder the light's unnatural and things look strange, when the city, and most likely the whole world, is imprisoned under this gigantic tent, cut off from the sun, moon and stars.

Why did I ever imagine that I was free? The truth is I couldn't be more thoroughly trapped. Those vast walls enclosing me in an unbroken circle have now assumed a more spectral aspect, and look more like mist. But this doesn't make them any less impenetrable, impassable. Not at all. Only too well I know that there's no way through them, that I shall never escape.

The thought of being shut in for ever drives me out of my senses, so that I try to bash down walls with my bare hands, tear at bricks with my nails, pick the mortar out. It's too ghastly. I'm not the sort of person who can live without seeing the sky. On the contrary, I have to look at it many times a day, I'm dying to be a part of it like the stars themselves. A cold finger of claustrophobia touches me icily. I can't be imprisoned like this. Somehow or other I must get out.

Suddenly on the edge of panic, I look round desperately for help. But of course I'm alone, as I always am. The pavements are deserted, there isn't a soul in sight. Once again I've been betrayed and abandoned; by the whole human race this time. Only the traffic continues to hurtle past, cascades of cars racing along the street in a ceaseless metallic flood.

Above the din of their engines louder crashes erupt all round. Avalanches of deafening noise explode in my ears like bombs. In all the thunderous booming roar I can distinguish the sobs of heartbroken children, the shrieks of tortured victims and addicts deprived of drugs, sadistic laughter, moronic cries, the moans of unsuccessful suicides —the whole catastrophe of this inhuman city, where the wolf-howl of ambulances and police cars rises perpetually from dark gullies between the enormous buildings.

Why am I locked in this nightmare of violence, isolation and cruelty? Since the universe only exists in my mind, I must have created the place, loathsome, foul as it is. I live alone in my mind, and alone I'm being crushed to suffocation, immured by the walls I have made. It's unbearable. I can't possibly live in this terrible, hideous, revolting creation of mine.

I can't die in it either, apparently. Demented, in utter frenzy, I rush madly up and down, hurl myself like a maniac into the traffic, bang my head with all my force against walls. Nothing changes. It makes no difference. The horror goes on just the same. It was enough that the world seemed to me vile and hateful for it to be so. And so it will remain, until I see it in a more favourable light—which means never.

So there's to be no end to my incarceration in this abominable, disgusting world. . . . My thoughts go round in circles. Mad with despair, I don't know what I'm doing, I can't remember or think any more. The terror of life imprisonment stupefies me, I feel it inside me like an intolerable pain. I only know that I must escape from this hell of hallucination and horror. I can't endure my atrocious prison a moment longer.

There's only one way of escape that I've ever discovered, and needless to say I haven't forgotten that.

So now I wave my arm frantically at a passing taxi, fall inside, and tell the man to drive to the old address.

A Visit

One hot night a leopard came into my room and lay down on the bed beside me. I was half asleep, and did not realize at first that it was a leopard. I seemed to be dreaming the sound of some large, soft-footed creature padding quietly through the house, the doors of which were wide open because of the intense heat. It was almost too dark to see the lithe, muscular shape coming into my room, treading softly on velvet paws, coming straight to the bed without hesitation, as if perfectly familiar with its position. A light spring, then warm breath on my arm, on my neck and shoulder, as the visitor sniffed me before lying down. It was not until later, when moonlight entering through the window revealed an abstract spotted design, that I recognized the form of an unusually large, handsome leopard stretched out beside me.

His breathing was deep though almost inaudible, he seemed to be sound asleep. I watched the regular contractions and expansions of the deep chest, admired the elegant relaxed body and supple limbs, and was confirmed in my conviction that the leopard is the most beautiful of all wild animals. In this particular specimen I noticed something singularly human about the formation of the skull, which was domed rather than flattened, as is generally

19

the case with the big cats, suggesting the possibility of superior brain development inside. While I observed him, I was all the time breathing his natural odour, a wild primeval smell of sunshine, freedom, moon and crushed leaves, combined with the cool freshness of the spotted hide, still damp with the midnight moisture of jungle plants. I found this non-human scent, surrounding him like an aura of strangeness, peculiarly attractive and stimulating.

My bed, like the walls of the house, was made of palm-leaf matting stretched over stout bamboos, smooth and cool to the touch, even in the great heat. It was not so much a bed as a room within a room, an open staging about twelve feet square, so there was ample space for the leopard as well as myself. I slept better that night than I had since the hot weather started, and he too seemed to sleep peacefully at my side. The close proximity of this powerful body of another species gave me a pleasant sensation I am at a loss to name.

When I awoke in the faint light of dawn, with the parrots screeching outside, he had already got up and left the room. Looking out, I saw him standing, statuesque, in front of the house on the small strip of ground I keep cleared between it and the jungle. I thought he was con-templating departure, but I dressed and went out, and he was still there, inspecting the fringe of the dense vegeta-tion, in which huge heavy hornbills were noisily flopping about.

I called him and fed him with some meat I had in the house. I hoped he would speak, tell me why he had come and what he wanted of me. But though he looked at me thoughtfully with his large, lustrous eyes, seeming to under-stand what I said, he did not answer, but remained silent

all day. I must emphasize that there was no hint of
obstinacy or hostility in his silence, and I did not resent
it. On the contrary, I respected him for his reserve; and,
as the silence continued unbroken, I gave up expecting to
hear his voice. I was glad of the pretext for using mine
and went on talking to him. He always appeared to listen
and understand me.

The leopard was absent during much of the day. I
assumed that he went hunting for his natural food; but
he usually came back at intervals, and seldom seemed to
be far away. It was difficult to see him among the trees,
even when he was quite close, the pattern of his protective spots blended so perfectly with the pattern of sun-
spots through savage branches. Only by staring with
concentrated attention could I distinguish him from his
background; he would be crouching there in a deep-shaded
glade, or lying extended with extraordinary grace along a
limb of one of the giant kowikawas, whose branch-structure
supports less robust trees, as well as countless creepers
and smaller growths. The odd thing was that, as soon as
I'd seen him, he invariably turned his head as if conscious
that I was watching. Once I saw him much further off,
on the beach, which is only just visible from my house.
He was standing darkly outlined against the water, gazing
out to sea; but even at this distance, his head turned in my
direction, though I couldn't possibly have been in his
range of vision. Sometimes he would suddenly come indoors and silently go all through the house at a quick trot,
unexpectedly entering one room after another, before he
left again with the same mysterious abruptness. At other
times he would lie just inside or outside, with his head
resting on the threshold, motionless except for his watchful
moving eyes, and the twitching of his sensitive nostrils in

response to stimuli which my less acute senses could not perceive.

His movements were always silent, graceful, dignified, sure; and his large, dark eyes never failed to acknowledge me whenever we met in our daily comings and goings.

I was delighted with my visitor, whose silence did not conceal his awareness of me. If I walked through the jungle to visit someone, or to buy food from the neighbouring village, he would appear from nowhere and walk beside me, but always stopped before a house was in sight, never allowing himself to be seen. Every night, of course, he slept on the bed at my side. As the weeks passed he seemed to be spending more time with me during the day, sitting or lying near me while I was working, now and then coming close to gaze attentively at what I was doing.

Then, without warning, he suddenly left me. This was how it happened. The rainy season had come, bringing cooler weather; there was a chill in the early morning air, when he returned to my room as I finished dressing, and leaned against me for a moment. He had hardly ever touched me in daylight, certainly never in that deliberate fashion. I took it to mean that he wished me to do something for him, and asked what it was. Silently he led the way out of the house, pausing to look back every few steps to see whether I was coming, and into the jungle. The stormy sky was heavily clouded, it was almost dark under the trees, from which great drops of last night's rain splashed coldly on my neck and bare arms. As he evidently wanted me to accompany him further, I said I would go back for a coat.

However, he seemed to be too impatient to wait, lunging forward with long, loping strides, his shoulders thrusting like steel pistons under the velvet coat, while I reluctantly followed. Torrential rain began streaming down, in five minutes the ground was a bog, into which my feet sank at each step. By now I was shivering, soaked to the skin, so I stopped and told him I couldn't go on any further. He turned his head and for a long moment his limpid eyes looked at me fixedly, with an expression I could not read. Then the beautiful head turned away, the muscles slid and bunched beneath patterned fur, as he launched himself in a tremendous leap through the shining curtain of raindrops, and was instantly hidden from sight. I walked home as fast as I could, and changed into dry clothes. I did not expect to see him again before evening, but he did not come back at all.

Nothing of any interest took place after the leopard's visit. My life resumed its former routine of work and trivial happenings. The rains came to an end, winter merged imperceptibly into spring. I took pleasure in the sun and the natural world. I felt sure the leopard meant to return, and often looked out for him, but throughout this period he never appeared. When the sky hung pure and cloudless over the jungle, many-coloured orchids began to flower on the trees. I went to see one or two people I knew; a few people visited me in my house. The leopard was never mentioned in our conversations.

The heat increased day by day, each day dawned glassily clear. The atmosphere was pervaded by the aphrodisiac perfume of wild white jasmine, which the girls wove into wreaths for their necks and hair. I painted some large new murals on the walls of my house, and started to make a terrace from a mosaic of coloured shells. For months I'd been expecting to see the leopard, but as time kept passing without a sign of him, I was gradually losing hope.

The season of oppressive heat came round in due course, and the house was left open all night. More than at any other time, it was at night, just before falling asleep, that I thought of the leopard, and, though I no longer believed it would happen, pretended that I'd wake to find him beside me again. The heat deprived me of energy, the progress of the mosaic was slow. I had never tried my hand at such work before, and being unable to calculate the total quantity of shells that would be required, I constantly ran out of supplies, and had to make tiring trips to the beach for more.

One day while I was on the shore, I saw, out to sea, a young man coming towards the land, standing upright on the crest of a huge breaker, his red cloak blowing out in the wind, and a string of pelicans solemnly flapping in line behind him. It was so odd to see this stranger, with his weird escort, approaching alone from the ocean on which no ships ever sailed, that my thoughts immediately connected him with the leopard : there must be some contact between them; perhaps he was bringing me news. As he got nearer, I shouted to him, called out greetings and questions, to which he replied. But because of the noise of the waves and the distance between us, I could not understand him. Instead of coming on to the beach to speak to me, he suddenly turned and was swept out to sea again, disappearing in clouds of spray. I was puzzled and disappointed. But I took the shells home, went on working as usual, and presently forgot the encounter.

Some time later, coming home at sunset, I was reminded of the young man of the sea by the sight of a pelican perched on the highest point of my roof. Its presence surprised me : pelicans did not leave the shore as a rule, I had never known one come as far inland as this. It

suddenly struck me that the bird must be something to do
with the leopard, perhaps bringing a message from him. To
entice it closer, I found a small fish in the kitchen, which
I put on the grass. The pelican swooped down at once,
and with remarkable speed and neatness, considering its
bulk, skewered the fish on its beak, and flew off with it.
I called out, strained my eyes to follow its flight; but only
caught a glimpse of the great wings flapping away from me
over the jungle trees, before the sudden black curtain of
tropical darkness came down with a rush.

Despite this inconclusive end to the episode, it revived
my hope of seeing the leopard again. But there were no
further developments of any description; nothing else
in the least unusual occurred.

It was still the season when the earth sweltered under
a simmering sky. In the afternoons the welcome trade wind
blew through the rooms and cooled them, but as soon as
it died down the house felt hotter than ever. Hitherto I
had always derived a nostalgic pleasure from recalling my
visitor; but now the memory aroused more sadness than
joy, as I had finally lost all hope of his coming back.

At last the mosaic was finished and looked quite impressive, a noble animal with a fine spotted coat and a
human head gazing proudly from the centre of the design.
I decided it needed to be enclosed in a border of yellow
shells, and made another expedition to the beach, where
the sun's power was intensified by the glare off the bright
green waves, sparkling as if they'd been sprinkled all over
with diamonds. A hot wind whistled through my hair,
blew the sand about, and lashed the sea into crashing
breakers, above which flocks of sea birds flew screaming,
in glistening clouds of spray. After searching for shells for
a while I straightened up, feeling almost dizzy with the

heat and the effort. It was at this moment, when I was dazzled by the violent colours and the terrific glare, that the young man I'd already seen reappeared like a mirage, the red of his flying cloak vibrating against the vivid emerald-green waves. This time, through a haze of shimmering brilliance, I saw that the leopard was with him, majestic and larger than life, moving as gracefully as if the waves were solid glass.

I called to him, and though he couldn't have heard me above the thundering of the surf, he turned his splendid head and gave me a long, strange, portentous look, just as he had that last time in the jungle, sparkling rainbows of spray now taking the place of rain. I hurried towards the edge of the water, then suddenly stopped, intimidated by the colossal size of the giant rollers towering over me. I'm not a strong swimmer, it seemed insane to challenge those enormous on-coming walls of water, which would certainly hurl me back contemptuously on to the shore with all my bones broken. Their exploding roar deafened me, I was half-blinded by the salt spray, the whole beach was a swirling, glittering dazzle, in which I lost sight of the two sea-borne shapes. And when my eyes brought them back into focus, they had changed direction, turned from the land, and were already a long way off, receding fast, diminishing every second, reduced to vanishing point by the hard, blinding brilliance of sun and waves.

Long after they'd disappeared, I stood there, staring out at that turbulent sea, on which I had never once seen any kind of boat, and which now looked emptier, lonelier, and more desolate than ever before. I was paralysed by depression and disappointment, and could hardly force myself to pick up the shells I'd collected and carry them home.

That was the last time I saw the leopard. I've heard nothing of him since that day, or of the young man. For a little while I used to question the villagers who lived by the sea, some of them said they vaguely remembered a man in a red cloak riding the water. But they always ended by becoming evasive, uncertain, and making contradictory statements, so that I knew I was wasting my time.

I've never said a word about the leopard to anyone. It would be difficult to describe him to these simple people, who can never have seen a creature even remotely like him, living here in the wilds as they do, far from zoos, circuses, cinemas and television. No carnivora, no large or ferocious beasts of any sort have ever inhabited this part of the world, which is why we can leave our houses open all night without fear.

The uneventful course of my life continues, nothing happens to break the monotony of the days. Sometime, I suppose, I may forget the leopard's visit. As it is I seldom think of him, except at night when I'm waiting for sleep to come. But, very occasionally he still enters my dreams, which disturbs me and makes me feel restless and sad. Although I never remember the dreams when I wake, for days afterwards they seem to weigh me down with the obscure bitterness of a loss which should have been prevented, and for which I am myself to blame.

Fog

I always liked to drive fast. But I wasn't driving as fast as usual that day, partly because it was foggy, but mainly because I felt calmly contented and peaceful, and there was no need to rush. The feeling was injected, of course. But it also seemed to have something to do with the fog and the windscreen wipers. I was alone, but the swinging wipers were keeping me company and acting as tranquillizers as they cleared their half-circles of glass, helping me to feel not quite there, as if I was driving the car in my sleep. The fog helped too, by blurring the world outside the windows, so that it looked vague and unreal.

These people looked as unreal as everything else. I'd just driven over a level-crossing when they appeared ahead, a group of long-haired, exotically-dressed teenagers, laughing and talking and singing as they wandered along hand in hand or with arms round each other's waists, all of them obviously on top of the world. In the ordinary way it would have annoyed me to see them straggling all over the road as if they owned it. I would have resented their being so sure of themselves, so relaxed and gay, when I often felt depressed, insecure and lonely, and had no one to talk to or laugh with. But this lot couldn't disturb me because they weren't real. I remained perfectly cool and

detached, even though they didn't attempt to get out of
the way, and actually signalled to me to stop.

I just looked indifferently at their silly faces surrounded
by all that idiotic hair in wet snake-like strands, every
grinning face wet and glistening with fog, every mouth
opening and shutting, with breath steaming out of it in
clouds. They reminded me of Japanese dragon-masks and
also of the subhuman nightmare mask-faces in some of
Ensor's paintings. These faces grimacing at me through
the fog had the same sort of slightly eerie repulsiveness of
masks, of walking and talking things, not really alive.
They'd have repelled me if they'd been human beings. But
as they were only dummies I felt nothing about them, my
indifference was unaffected. It was just that I would have
preferred not to be looking at them.

I had no intention of giving any of them a lift, naturally. However, as they wouldn't get off the road, I
automatically moved my foot from the accelerator towards
the brake. But then I thought, why? They weren't real.
None of this was real. I wasn't really here, so they couldn't
be either. It was absurd to treat them as real live people.
So back went my foot on to the accelerator again. They
were just a collection of disagreeable masks I was looking
at in my sleep. I was absolutely detached and cool, there
wasn't a trace of emotion involved, no feeling whatever.

One dummy came up too close to me. Through the
fog, I saw the painted mask-face opposite mine, staring
straight at me, mouth and eyes opening wider and wider
in a grotesque caricature of incredulity. Then there was a
bump, and I gripped the wheel hard with both hands as
if this was what had to be done to avert some disaster—
precisely what disaster seemed immaterial.

The incident was unduly prolonged. Strange caterwaulings went on interminably and indistinct shapes fell about. When at last it was over, I drove on as if nothing had happened. Nothing had really. I didn't give it a thought, there was nothing to think about. I just went on driving calmly and carefully in the fog, the windscreen wipers swinging regularly to and fro, promoting that peaceful dream-like sense of not being present.

An abrupt apparition loomed up at a foggy corner, slewed right across the road. The idea of avoiding a crash between our two unrealities never entered my head: some reflex action must have made me swerve at the last moment and scrape past a huge articulated lorry. Ignoring the driver's shouts, I drove on again, doing thirty-five to forty, not more, not thinking of anything in particular, the wipers swinging, the fog making everything vague.

It was pleasantly soothing to feel so detached, so tranquil. Then it began to get boring. Everything went on and on: the fog, the windscreen wipers, my driving. It was as if I didn't know how to stop the car, and would have to drive till the tank was dry, or all roads came to an end.

So I was quite relieved when the police car stopped me. I got out and stood in the road and asked what they wanted. They could see for themselves that I wasn't drunk: and I certainly hadn't been driving dangerously. A sergeant asked me to come to the station, and I agreed. It was all the same to me where I was, as I wasn't there really. I might as well be at a police station as anywhere else. They wanted to search the car and I made no objection. There was nothing to be found in it, the syringe and the rest of the stuff was in my bag. While I was waiting for them to finish I looked out of the window. It was dusk now outside. I watched the lights come on and shine yellow in the foggy street.

An inspector interviewed me alone in a small, cold, brightly-lit room with notices in small print on the walls and two bicycles leaning against them. We sat on hard wooden chairs on opposite sides of a desk covered in black formica. I kept my coat collar turned up. He was a big man whose very square shoulders somehow looked artificial. I thought of those dummies children make with coat-hangers and sticks and cushions stuffed inside clothes. His face was an imitation, a mask made of cardboard or papier mâché, with green eyes painted on. In the strong light I saw these eyes watching me vacuously, without any expression, gazing blankly at my hair, my watch, my suede coat.

I looked back at them calmly, indifferently, wondering what they were seeing, if anything. Obviously he wasn't real. He was just a sham, I was seeing him in my sleep, so he couldn't disturb me. That was all I was thinking. I was absolutely cool and detached, there wasn't a trace of emotion involved, not even when he asked if I'd witnessed the accident at the level-crossing.

The room was so cold that his breath steamed out in front of him while he was speaking. For a second I seemed to be watching the steaming mouths of those other masks, bobbing about in the fog like horrid Halloween pumpkins with candles smoking inside. His boring proletarian face looked unreal and subhuman like theirs. He had the same slightly weird repulsiveness of a talking thing, not in any way human. He would have repelled me if he'd been real. But he was only a dummy, an ersatz man, so he couldn't affect my detachment any more than they could. I felt nothing whatever about him. I was indifferent.

It was just that I'd have preferred not to be sitting there facing him. I said 'No, I didn't see anything.' I had no intention of telling him, naturally. Not that there was anything to tell. None of this was real. It couldn't really be happening.

'You may be able to help us in our investigations.'

I didn't know what to say to this, so I remained silent. How could I possibly help if I hadn't seen what took place? He felt in one pocket, then in another, brought out a packet of Players and offered it to me. His hands were big, square, used-looking, like a working man's. 'No thanks. I don't smoke.' I sniffed with distaste the strong, rather stale smell of the Virginian tobacco.

'What, no vices?' He almost smiled, momentarily; I wondered why. He was pretending, putting on some sort of act. I looked indifferently, silently, at his mass-produced nonentity's face. There was no gleam of light, no life, in his eyes, they were flat green stones, devoid of intelligence or expression. I leaned my elbows on the desk. The situation was prolonging itself unduly. It had become boring. I looked at my watch.

A policewoman brought in a tray, put it down on the desk, and went out again. I took the thick white cup the inspector held out to me, and drank some of the tea, or it might have been coffee. The fog was starting to make my throat slightly sore.

'Do you want one of these?' I looked from his artisan's hands to the plate of plain dry biscuits and shook my head. He took one himself, broke it in half and swallowed it in two mouthfuls. I put the white cup down on the desk.

He said, 'Someone has been killed at the level-crossing.'

Three deep horizontal frown lines appeared on his fore-

head. His eyes were screwed up and half-shut. For a second
I again saw the teenage masks floating about in the fog.
One came too close and looked me straight in the face
with a ludicrously exaggerated expression of amazement or
disbelief. The mask-face across the desk was frowning at
me. I knew he was waiting for me to say something, but
there was nothing to say. A mask had been put out of
circulation. So what? A mask wasn't human. It was
meaningless, unimportant. The whole thing was unreal.

He had re-filled his cup, steam was rising from it.
Through the steam, his stereotyped imitation face floated
in front of me as if in fog, the green eyes, now wide open,
staring straight at me, but blankly, perhaps unseeing, they
looked almost blind. His square shoulders loomed through
the fog, he was a dummy made of stuffed clothes and
umbrellas, not real. Since he wasn't a human being I could
look at him without feeling, with perfect indifference. It
was just that I didn't want to look at him. I turned my
head.

The fog was thickening outside as evening came on. I
felt the rawness of it in my throat. Outside the window,
fog pressed closely against the glass. For a second I felt
trapped in a cold cell surrounded by fog. But I wasn't here
really. Nothing about the situation was real, so the room
couldn't be. The solid look of the walls was an illusion;
in reality they consisted of empty space, a field of force
between particles in a boundless void. Still, I would have
preferred to be somewhere else.

I still felt peaceful, but now I'd begun to be dimly
aware of some distant threat to peace. I put it out of my
mind as I heard him say, 'Think! Are you quite sure
you saw nothing unusual on the road? No one who'd
been injured?'

B

'I've told you, I didn't see anything at all.'

'But the lorry driver says you passed him directly after the accident. So surely you must have seen something.'

His voice sounded sharper. I had the idea that he glanced at me sharply, almost as if he was really alive. But when my eyes got back to him the mask was the same, with the eyes half-shut again as before, painted flat on the frowning fake-face.

'What lorry driver?' I asked. 'I don't know what you're talking about. Can't you see it's all a mistake and I'm not the person you want?'

I looked at my watch again. He hadn't answered me. I watched him start looking through a small notebook in a shiny black cover. I was still coolly indifferent, insulated by detachment. But a disturbing doubt was creeping in somewhere. It was beginning to seem as if the situation might never end at all : and I wasn't entirely sure my detachment would last out an interminable situation. Watching him turn the pages of the small book, I was again aware of a far off threat, a black cloud on a remote horizon.

'The driver took the car's registration number.' He had found what he wanted and now read out some figures to me. 'That's the number of your car, isn't it? So you see there can't be any mistake. And it is you we want.' He moved abruptly, leaned right over the desk, bringing his face so near mine that instinctively I drew back from the smell of stale smoke and infrequently-cleaned heavy clothes, mixed with a faint sharper, sicklier smell of alcohol.

'Suppose you start telling me the truth now.' The tone of his voice was surprisingly new and peremptory. His empty expressionless eyes had suddenly come to life. His

dull dummy-policeman's face looked unexpectedly real
and threatening.

I could feel the black cloud coming closer as I watched
him get up and walk round the desk, his gaze and movements now permeated by a chilly deliberation. He stood
over me ominously, his big, square, worker's hands right
in my line of vision, yellowish against the dark uniform,
ominously powerful; his padded-looking shoulders bending slightly, ominously, towards me, and much too close.
I didn't want to see him. I looked round him, out of the
window, instead.

I could smell the fog, I could taste it, it rasped my
throat. Outside, daylight was going fast. The street was
completely deserted. I heard no traffic noises from other
streets. A low dirty foggy ceiling pressed down from
above, dingily reflecting the lights of the town. The fog
itself was thicker than ever, and had turned a dense, bilious
yellow, like vomit. The window panes failed to keep it
out of the room. Horizontal lines of fog hung visibly in
the air, the lights shone dull yellow through them.

For a moment I felt trapped again, this time by something darker and deadlier than the fog. I still wasn't quite
there. But my injected tranquillity was gradually wearing
off, and, even without being fully identified with the situation, it was becoming difficult to ignore the existence of
some sort of threat somewhere. I suspected that I was
about to lose my detachment, and then everything would
become intolerable.

So, after all, this did somehow concern me, although I
couldn't see how, on account of the fog. The fog was
everywhere, it was inside my head. I seemed not to understand quite what had been happening . . . not to remember
. . . it was as if I didn't quite grasp what was going on. I

had the impression of having lost touch, lost control of events, while all the time a black cloud of something like poison gas was surging towards me.

I suddenly wanted to escape then, before it was too late. I knew I must take immediate action to extricate myself from the situation. But I couldn't do this as long as things seemed unreal and I wasn't really here, so first I had to stop feeling absent and disconnected. All of a sudden, I urgently wanted to wake up, not just sit here in my sleep, but be really here, instead of nowhere.

However, it seemed to be too late already, I saw that there was no escape from the situation. The black cloud filled the room, I was breathing in poison as well as fog, inhaling a poisonous mixture of stale smoke and alcohol smell.

Then I looked round, and instantaneously stopped wanting to wake up. The last thing I wanted was to be awake here, when I saw the inspector still standing horribly close, no longer a lifeless dummy, a commonplace cardboard mask, but a sinister human being with frightening powers over me, whose green watching eyes had turned cold, ruthless, piercing, in a hard face now ominously alive and real, accusatory, unmistakably menacing.

All I wanted then was for everything to go on as before, so that I could stay deeply asleep, and be no more than a hole in space, not here or anywhere at all, for as long as possible, preferably for ever.

Experimental

I like this red and white room because it's entirely mine, mine alone, I don't share it with anyone, I planned it and chose its colours. White, tranquil, serene and cool, to remind me of the aloof, immaculate, snow-covered mountains; red for contrast, for love and roses, for danger, violence, blood.

This bed is comfortable and good to look at. It's a good place to be because I'm alone in it. Why must the wrong man always be in the bed? I often used to think in the past. At one time it was Torquil with his lack of technique; followed by others whose methods were equally non-erotic. And now there is Oblomov, who ignores my existence all day and leaves me alone at night, and yet wishes to visit my bed when he returns in the small hours, so that I had to get the psychiatrist to insist on our sleeping in separate rooms in order to keep him away. How presumptuous of him to expect a welcome from me after behaving with such unkindness.

He seems to think he can treat me abominably, and still be entitled to a place in my bed, although I've told him he's ceased to attract me. In fact, I find him downright repulsive these days.

Yet it was once my pleasure to please him. And, in a

way, I still seem attached to him, even now; though perhaps my attachment is more to the sexual act, as it used to take place between us, than it is to him.

When sexual pleasure is associated with understanding affection, and there is some affinity between those concerned, a mystique is created which persists even in totally different situations.

I wonder if it would work with another person—if those remembered pleasures would revive spontaneously, and the emotions he aroused in the first place repeat themselves automatically with somebody else? I think I will make a small experiment to find out whether this is the case. It will at least be a way of passing the time. And even an unsuccessful experiment is to be preferred to the emptiness and isolation I have to endure every night in these silent and lonely rooms. No doubt that good-looking Scandinavian I've met a few times would oblige by co-operating in the experiment with me. I shall take the first opportunity of getting things started.

'Have you had lots of lovers?' he asked without looking at me. 'Do you always let them come here?' I didn't answer. He was prowling up and down my room, peering at everything inquisitively and suspiciously, like an animal just let out in a strange place after a journey. 'Isn't it risky —even with separate rooms? Aren't you afraid your husband will find out?' I was bored. He asked far too many questions. I watched him prowl, saw that he was frowning, nervous as a cat. When he lifted one hand and in an absent sort of way, started chewing the tips of the fingers, the situation suddenly seemed distasteful, I wished I hadn't let myself in for it. I wanted to stop the whole thing before it was too late, but for some reason I couldn't make the effort.

Outside the window, against the green sweep of the hills, the tops of the elm trees were full of untidy nests. I knew this view intimately, looked at it many times every day. Only now I wasn't seeing the view itself, but something more like a realistic painting of it. This made everything seem rather queer. Nothing out there looked quite real.

The young man wasn't quite real either. I half-expected him to vanish while I was looking the other way. But when I turned my head, there he was, still prowling about like a cat, a young fellow I'd met perhaps half a dozen times, a complete stranger. I must have been out of my mind. Of course love-making with him couldn't possibly be anything like those remembered occasions for which a special affinity was required. This was just a stupid mistake on my part, not even an experiment, just something I had to get through.

'Hadn't we better pull the curtains?' He was frowning more than ever, his hand was already on the stiff red felt folds. I found his nervousness irritating, he should have controlled it. 'We're miles from anywhere. And no one could possibly see in, even if there was anybody to look.' It seemed beyond me to add, as I meant to, 'But call it off if you're scared.' He gazed at me dubiously, and then began, slowly and awkwardly, to take off his jacket, keeping well back, away from the window.

I went into the bathroom, shut the door, got out the syringe and filled it. The needle went in at once, easily and painlessly. I looked at myself in the glass, examined the scars on my thighs, wondered if a stranger would be repelled when he saw them first. Not that I cared about this one. They didn't show very much anyhow, no more than the scars acne leaves sometimes on people's faces.

When I re-entered the bedroom it was full of subdued ruby light. 'So you did pull the curtains.' Perhaps it was just as well, he wouldn't be able to see the marks now. He had undressed completely and was lying flat on the bed, from which he had not removed the bedspread. Waiting a moment for the injection to take effect, I observed the body of this stranger. The flesh was very white and unexpectedly hairy; the hairs, unexpectedly black and wiry, stood up like fir trees in snow. Then I noticed his clothes, folded on one of the chairs, jacket and trousers draped neatly over the back. He clearly had some appreciation of order, so why hadn't he thought of taking the bedspread off?

'Come along. Why are you standing there?' He stretched out his hand, but let it drop before it touched me. I got on to the bed beside him, and leaning against the padded headboard, looked at the line of firs marching above his navel to meet those marching in single file down from his sternum. Fir forests spread out over his chest and thighs. It seemed odd that a northerner should have such black hair. But then everything seemed odd. Now he was silently gazing at me in a peculiar way, as if he expected me to behave differently. I wondered what I was supposed to do. At the same time I had the feeling none of this could be real.

'What's the matter? I shan't get pregnant, if you're thinking of that. Or don't you want to go on?' My impulse was still to call off the whole thing, but the general sense of unreality acted as a deterrent. Besides, it seemed to be too late already, now that we'd got undressed. He said, 'Being in this house makes me nervous. About your husband, I mean. Suppose he suddenly walks in?'

'He won't.'

'How can you be sure?'

'Because he never comes back before two or three in the morning.'

'Why not? What an extraordinary thing . . . . What on earth does he do all that time? He's not working at night, is he?' I said nothing. His questions got on my nerves. The mixture of apprehension and curiosity was exasperating, or would have been, if I hadn't felt so detached and bored and outside the situation. As it couldn't be stopped, I wanted to get it over as quickly as possible. It seemed nothing to do with me. But I tried to involve myself by taking hold of his hand and moving it around for a while. It was a hard, bony hand, with hairs sprouting out of the back like black wires.

Then I left things to him, and he gripped me hard but with expertise. It was better than I expected. For a second I almost managed to feel involved. Then the situation slipped away from me and once more became unreal, I was once more left somewhere outside it. He was panting and heaving, making muffled noises a bit like a seal I'd heard barking once in a cave on the shore. When he was finished, I observed this naked stranger stretched out on top of the crumpled bedspread. One leg was bent at the knee, his hairy, white-fleshed body looked unrelated to the strong-looking legs emerging from it like pillars at different angles. He rolled over and propped himself on his elbow.

'Was I too quick for you?' he asked anxiously. 'It can happen occasionally, if I'm at all nervous.' His anxiety appeared to be genuine. It struck me as slightly funny, as if he expected me to circulate a report on his sexual performance. Evidently he had a reputation in this field which had to be kept up. I assured him that it had been O.K. and he seemed relieved.

I watched his legs swing over the edge of the bed and hoist him on to his feet beside it. They seemed more expressive than his good-looking foreign face, where a rather meaningless smile had become fixed, probably due, it occurred to me, to some embarrassment for which I was responsible. But he was merely a stranger, nothing to do with me. I couldn't bother about him. The bedspread was a complete mess. It was a fitted one, made of white felt with a sign of Aries in the same red as the curtains. Now it would have to go to the cleaners.

While he was running the water in the bathroom I looked out at the elm trees against the green sweep of the hills, their tops full of old untidy nests, and many of their yellowing leaves already down on the ground. Nothing much was left in the garden but a few roses among gangrenous blotches of purple and yellow autumnal flowers. I was looking out at a colour photograph, real and yet not real.

I turned on the hot tap and sniffed the scent of the soap I'd brought with me from abroad. It was unobtainable here. There were only a few tablets left. I must be more careful of it in future, not let anyone else use it. As I was drying myself I looked out of the window. The view from this one was slightly different. I watched a few sleep-walking cows slowly cross the field with the elms. They weren't real cows, more like wooden toys; no, like model cows, too realistic for toys or for the real thing. Higher up, the beech woods, still dusty yellow-green, fitted down in neat caps over the tops of the hills. They would soon turn bronze, then gold and finally misty purple when all the leaves had come down. The end of the summer made me feel vaguely sad.

The young man had drawn back the bedroom curtains, letting in daylight again. Standing there in his socks and trousers, he was putting on a dark blue shirt sprinkled with small white flowers. I tried to think of something to say, but my mind was blank. No communication seemed possible. I preferred him in his clothes, he looked more human, more like a person with whom one might conceivably, though improbably, have some slight contact, sometime. All the same, I still had nothing to say to him.

'What sort of a man is your husband?' He was gazing at me curiously again. 'Why does he go out and leave you alone like this? Doesn't he ever suspect you of being unfaithful? Or does he know and not mind?'

I had no intention of answering silly questions. I slid open the door of the built-in wardrobe, got out a silk suit and started to put it on. I'd already agreed to go out to dinner with him somewhere. I wondered why. It would only prolong the boredom. He was only a stranger who meant nothing to me and kept asking annoying questions. Then I remembered the silent loneliness of the house after dark and no voice ever speaking, no light to be seen anywhere. His arm came forward to help me on with the jacket, and I saw the line of black firs marching up the snow slope, the wiry fir trees crowding under his sleeve.

I watched him take out a comb and stand in front of the looking-glass, carefully combing the long hair forward over his forehead, and back in black curls on his neck. Then he picked up my silver hand-mirror and looked at the back of his head, twisting it from side to side, touching the curls into place. They looked as rigid and permanent as if they were made of wire. He took a long time to arrange his hair. It was a performance. I

almost felt I ought to applaud at the end. Suddenly I
saw him as an adolescent, he suddenly seemed years
younger than I was, though just as much a stranger as
ever.

I combed my own hair and did my face. The girl in the
glass looked reasonably attractive, but she was nothing to
do with me, so it made no difference. She was just a
reflection, a no–thing, not me at all. None of this seemed
to affect me in any way. I only felt bored and sad and
beyond it all.

We went down the stairs together, I first and he following. I could feel him staring hard at the back of my head
the whole time.

'You have beautiful hair,' he said, reaching out to stroke
it; but let his hand fall without achieving the gesture. 'Of
course everyone tells you that.' He was a total stranger.
I must have been out of my mind. I left him alone in
the sitting-room while I fetched the drinks.

I didn't hurry. Indeed, I was deliberately slow. Endless
vistas of boredom extended, although there was a choice :
either the boredom of this stranger and of his questions;
or else the lonely and silent house. So perhaps there was
no real choice, after all.

I put the glasses and bottles on to a tray before I went
to get the ice out of the refrigerator. Then, when I
turned round again he was behind me, he'd found his
way into the kitchen and was prowling about, examining
everything, exactly as he'd done upstairs.

'You must eat a lot of fruit.' He stopped in front of
a big bowl of lemons and oranges on the table, and his
pleasantly foreign face looked at me with a new expression.
His smile was no longer fixed or meaningless, but had
suddenly come alive rather nicely, in a way that made him

seem suddenly likable. At that moment I would have liked to like him, if there had been any connection, if any of this had been real.

Dusk was falling as we went out to his long red sports car, which was very low, very smart, very fast. 'How do you like her?' he asked, apparently confident that I would approve of the powerful shiny red monster. In return for his likable moment, I expressed the required admiration. Distances had already begun to look dark and dense, the white gates at the end of the drive stood out against blackish laurels. I could feel in the air the melancholy of approaching autumn; and yet at the same time, I felt disconnected, outside everything. He drove too fast in the narrow lanes, steering with one hand most of the time, holding a lighted cigarette in the other, showing off for my benefit. There would probably be hours more of this sort of thing.

The wind tore at us, instantly snatched the smoke from his mouth. I tied a scarf round my head and asked where we were going.

'To The Mitre.'

'All that way?'

I didn't want to go so far, it was about forty miles. It would take far too long. The whole thing was becoming far too much of a bore. I wanted to say, Take me home instead. But I thought of the nocturnal loneliness of the house behind us, and what I actually said was, 'Why not go to The Spread Eagle? It's much nearer, and the food's just as good.'

He glanced at me briefly, the nice smile turned sly. 'We'll be safer at The Mitre.' Evidently he didn't want anyone he knew to see us together.

I said the first thing that came into my head. 'This

car's too conspicuous for a Don Juan.' He giggled as if
I'd paid him a compliment, which had not been my intention. The giggle made him seem adolescent again. I felt
a thousand years old.

I couldn't be bothered to argue about where we went
for dinner. I knew I ought to make conversation, but we
didn't connect, there was nothing on earth to say. It made
no sense to be half-lying down in a low seat at the side
of a stranger with black wire curls on his neck. Darkness
thickened the air, the hedges streamed past, black and
close. When he leaned forward, flicking the lights on
and off, the curls resting on the back of his neck didn't
move, but remained as immobile and perfect as if they
were really tightly-curled springs of black wire. I wondered
what he was thinking, if he did think. I couldn't see what
satisfaction he could be getting out of the situation.

His eyes slid sideways, glancing at me, glittering momentarily in the light, the pupils gliding towards me like
sly little fish.

'Why won't you tell me about your husband?' I was
silent, I wasn't going to answer his questions. It was exasperating that he kept on asking them. 'You're not still
in love with him, are you?' The nice smiling look had
gone from his face as completely as if he'd discarded a
pleasant mask. Now he was starting to frown and look
nervous again. 'You wouldn't be unfaithful if you loved
him, would you?' Again I caught the curious gleam of his
sly darting minnow-eyes. 'And it doesn't seem as if he's
in love with you, leaving you so much alone . . . . Where
does he go in the evenings? To see friends? Round the
pubs? Or what?'

'I've no idea,' I replied coolly. The coolness was lost
upon him.

'But surely he must say what he's up to when he stays out so late—don't you ever ask him?' I didn't answer, just made a vague, bored, non-committal sound. He was growing more tense and nervous each moment. Frowning more deeply, he abruptly threw out the cigarette he'd just lighted, suddenly gripping the wheel with both hands. 'He wouldn't go as far as The Mitre, would he?'

This undisguised anxiety seemed rather contemptible, and at the same time somehow insulting. He should have concealed it. 'I've no idea,' I repeated coldly. The coldness made no impression, didn't register with him. He was entirely self-absorbed, scowling, his lips tightly pressed together. I could hardly believe I'd ever thought he looked likeable, even for a second. Now everything about him repelled me. I couldn't stand the sight of him, and looked out at the black flying hedges and shadowy roadside trees. They were the same trees and hedges I'd already been seeing for miles. Only now I wasn't seeing the dark road scene itself, but something more like a film version of it. This made everything seem rather queer. Nothing out there looked quite real.

The young man wasn't quite real either. I half-expected him to have vanished when I turned my head. But there he was, still sitting beside me, now lifting one hand off the wheel and chewing the tips of the fingers in an absent sort of way.

The situation had all along been irritating and boring. Now it suddenly became so distasteful I couldn't stand any more of it. I must have been out of my mind to involve myself with a young fellow I'd only met about half a dozen times, a complete stranger, really.

Except that of course I was not involved, none of this was real, it didn't concern me. And, from some remote point of dissociation, millions of miles away, I heard my depersonalized voice saying:

'I don't want to go on any further. Please take me back now.'

World of Heroes

I try not to look at the stars. I can't bear to see them. They make me remember the time when I used to look at them and think, I'm alive, I'm in love and I'm loved. I only really lived that part of my life. I don't feel alive now. I don't love the stars. They never loved me. I wish they wouldn't remind me of being loved.

I was slow in starting to live at all. It wasn't my fault. If there had ever been any kindness I would not have suffered from a delayed maturity. If so much apprehension had not been instilled into me, I shouldn't have been terrified to leave my solitary unwanted childhood in case something still worse was waiting ahead. However, there was no kindness. The nearest approach to it was being allowed to sit on the back seats of the big cars my mother drove about in with her different admirers. This was in fact no kindness at all. I was taken along to lend an air of respectability. The two in front never looked round or paid the slightest attention to me, and I took no notice of them. I sat for hours and hours and for hundreds of miles inventing endless fantasies at the back of large and expensive cars.

The frightful slowness of a child's time. The interminable years of inferiority and struggling to win a kind word that is never spoken. The torment of self-accusation, thinking one must be to blame. The bitterness of longed for affection bestowed on indifferent strangers. What future could have been worse? What could have been done to me to make me afraid to grow up out of such a childhood?

Later on, when I saw things more in proportion, I was always afraid of falling back into that ghastly black isolation of an uncomprehending, solitary, over-sensitive child, the worst fate I could imagine.

My mother disliked and despised me for being a girl. From her I got the idea that men were a superior breed, the free, the fortunate, the splendid, the strong. My small adolescent adventures and timid experiments with boys who occasionally gave me rides on the backs of their motor-bikes, confirmed this. All heroes were automatically masculine. Men are kinder than women; they could afford to be. They were also fierce, unpredictable, dangerous animals : one had to be constantly on guard against them.

My feeling for high-powered cars presumably came from my mother too. Periodically, ever since I can remember, the craving has come over me to drive and drive, from one country to another, in a fast car. Hearing people talk about danger and death on the roads seems ludicrous, laughable. To me, a big car is a very safe refuge, and the only means of escape from all the ferocious cruel forces lurking in life and in human beings. Its metal body surrounds me like magic armour, inside which I'm invulnerable. Everybody I meet in the outside world treats me in the same contemptuous, heartless way, discrediting what I do, refusing to admit my existence. Only the man in the car is different. Even the first time I drive with him, I feel that he appreciates, understands me; I know I can

make him love me. The car is a small speeding substitute
world, just big enough for us both. A sense of intimacy
is generated, a bond created between us. At once I start
to love him a little. Occasionally it's the car I love first:
the car can attract me to the man. When we are driving
together, the three of us form one unit. We grow into each
other. I forget about loneliness and inferiority, I feel fine.

In the outside world catastrophe always threatens. The
news is always bad. Life tears into one like a mad rocket
off course. The only hope of escaping is in a racing car.

At last I reached the age of freedom and was considered
adult; but still my over-prolonged adolescence made me
look less than my age. X, a young American with a
2.6 litre Alfa Romeo and lots of money, took me for
fifteen or sixteen. When I told him I was twenty-one, he
burst out laughing, called me a case of retarded development, seemed to be making fun of me in a cruel way. I
was frightened, ran away from him, travelled around with
some so-called friends with whom I was hopelessly bored.
After knowing X, they seemed insufferably dull, mediocre,
conventional. Obsessed by longing for him and his car, I
sent a telegram asking him to meet us. As soon as I'd
done it, I grew feverish with excitement and dread, finally
felt convinced the message would be ignored. How idiotic
to invite such a crushing rejection. I should never survive the disappointment and shame.

I was shaking all over when we got to the place. It was
evening. I hid in the shadows, kept my eyes down so as
not to see him—not to see that he wasn't there. Then he
was coming towards us. He shook hands with the others
one by one, leaving me to the last. I thought, he wants
to humiliate me. He's no more interested in me than he
is in them. Utterly miserable, I wanted to rush off and

lose myself in the dark. Suddenly he said my name, said he was driving me to another town, said goodbye to the rest so abruptly that they seemed to stand there, suspended, amazed, for the instant before I forgot their existence. He had taken hold of my arm, and was walking me rapidly to his car. He installed me in the huge, docile, captivating machine, and we shot away, the stars spinning loops of white fire all over the sky as we raced along the deserted roads.

That was how it began. I always think gratefully of X, who introduced me to the world of heroes.

The race track justifies tendencies and behaviour which would be condemned as antisocial in other circumstances. Risks encountered nowhere else but in war are a commonplace of the racing drivers' existence. Knowing they may be killed any day, they live in a wartime atmosphere of recklessness, camaraderie and heightened perception. The contrast of their light-hearted audacity and their sombre, sinister, menacing background gave them a personal glamour I found irresistible. They were all attractive to me, heroes, the bravest men in the world. Vaguely, I realized that they were also psychopaths, misfits, who played with death because they'd been unable to come to terms with life in the world. Their games could only end badly : few of them survived more than a few years. They were finished, anyhow, at thirty-five, when their reactions began to slow down, disqualifying them for the one thing they did so outstandingly well. They preferred to die before this happened.

Whether they lived or died, tragedy was waiting for them, only just round the corner, and the fact that they had so little time added to their attraction. It also united them in a peculiar, almost metaphysical way, as though something of all of them was in each individual. I thought of them as a sort of brotherhood, dedicated to their fatal profession of speed.

They all knew one another, met frequently, often lived in the same hotels. Their life was strictly nomadic. None of them had, or wanted to have, a place of his own to live in, even temporarily, far less a permanent home. The demands of their work made any kind of settled existence impossible. Only a few got married, and these marriages always came unstuck very quickly. The wives were jealous of the group feeling, they could not stand the strain, the eternal separation, the homelessness.

I had never had a home, and, like the drivers, never wanted one. But wherever I stayed with them was my proper place, and I felt at home there. All my complicated emotions were shut inside hotel rooms, like boxes inside larger ones. A door, a window, a looking-glass, impersonal walls. The door and the window opened only on things that had become unreal, the mirror only revealed myself. I felt protected, shut away from the world as I was in a car, safe in my retreat.

Although, after winning a race, they became for a short time objects of adulation and public acclaim, these men were not popular; the rest of humanity did not understand them. Their clannishness, their flippant remarks and casual manners were considered insulting; their unconventional conduct judged as immoral. The world seemed not to see either the careless elegance that appealed to me, or their strict aristocratic code, based on absolute loyalty to each other, absolute professional integrity, absolute fearlessness.

I loved them for being somehow above and apart from the general gregarious mass of mankind, born adventurers, with a breezy disrespect for authority. Perhaps they felt I was another misfit, a rebel too. Or perhaps they were intrigued or amused by the odd combination of my excessively youthful appearance and wholly pessimistic intelligence. At all events, they received me as no other social group could ever have done—conventions, families, finances would have prevented it. Straightaway, they accepted my presence among them as perfectly natural, adopted me as a sort of mascot. They were regarded as wild, irresponsible daredevils; but they were the only people I'd ever trusted. I was sure that, unlike all the others I'd known, they would not let me down.

Their code prohibited jealousy or any bad feeling. Unpleasant emotional situations did not arise. Finding that I was safe among them, I perceived that it was unnecessary to be on my guard any longer. Their attitude was at the same time flattering and matter of fact. They were considerate without any elaborate chivalry, which would have embarrassed me, and they displayed a frank, if restrained, physical interest, quite willing, apparently, to love me for as long or short a time as I liked. When my affair with A was finally over, I simply got into B's car, and that was that. It all seemed exceedingly simple and civilized.

The situation was perfect for me. They gave me what I had always wanted but never had : a background, true friends. They were kind in their unsentimental race track way, treated me as one of themselves, shared with me their life histories and their cynical jokes, listened to me with attention, but did not press me to talk. I sewed on buttons for them, checked hotel and garage accounts, acted as unskilled mechanic, looked after them if they were injured in crashes or caught influenza.

At last I felt wanted, valued, as I'd longed to be all my

life. At last I belonged somewhere, had a place, was some use in the world. For the very first time I understood the meaning of happiness, and it was easy for me to be truly in love with each of them. I could hardly believe I wasn't dreaming. It was incredible; but it was true, it was really happening. I never had time now to think or to get depressed, I was always in a car with one of them. I went on all the long rallies, won Grand Prix races, acted as co-driver or passenger as the occasion required. I loved it all, the speed, the exhaustion, the danger. I loved rushing down icy roads at ninety miles an hour, spinning round three times, and continuing non-stop without even touching the banked-up snow.

This was the one beautiful period of my life, when I drove all over the world, saw all its countries. The affection of these men, who risked their lives so casually, made me feel gay and wonderfully alive, and I adored them for it. By liking me, they had made the impossible happen. I was living a real fairy tale.

This miraculous state of affairs lasted for several years, and might have gone on some time longer. But, beyond my euphoria, beyond the warm lighthearted atmosphere they generated between them, the sinister threat in the background was always waiting. Disaster loomed over them like a circle of icy mountains, implacably drawing nearer : they'd developed a special attitude in self-defence. Because crashes and constant danger made each man die many times, they spoke of death as an ordinary event, for which the carelessness or recklessness of the individual was wholly responsible. Nobody ever said, 'Poor old Z's had it,' but, 'Z asked for it, the crazy bastard, never more than one jump ahead of the mortuary.' Their jargon had a brutal sound to outsiders. But, by speaking derisively of the victim, they deprived death of terror, made it seem something he could easily have avoided.

Without conscious reflection, I took it for granted that, when the time came, I would die on the track, like my friends : and this very nearly happened. The car crashed and turned four somersaults before it burst into flames, and the driver and the other passengers were killed instantly. I had the extreme bad luck to be dragged out of the blazing wreckage only three-quarters dead. Apparently my case was a challenge to the doctors of several hospitals, who, for the next two years, worked with obstinate persistence to save my life, while I persistently tried to discard it. I used to look in their cold, clinical eyes with loathing and helpless rage. They got their way in the end, and discharged me. I was pushed out again into the hateful world, alone, hardly able to walk, and disfigured by burns.

The drivers loyally kept in touch, wrote and sent presents to the hospitals, came to see me whenever they could. It was entirely my own fault that, as the months dragged on, the letters became fewer, the visits less and less frequent, until they finally ceased. I didn't want them to be sorry for me or to feel any obligation. I was sure my scarred face must repel them, so I deliberately drove them away.

I couldn't possibly go back to them : I had no heart, no vitality, for the life I'd so much enjoyed. I was no longer the gay, adventurous girl they had liked. All the same, if one of them had really exerted himself to persuade me, I might. . . . That nobody made this special effort, or showed a desire for further intimacy, confirmed my conviction that I had become repulsive. Although there was a possible alternative explanation. At the time of the crash, I had been in love with the man who was driving, and hadn't yet reached the stage of singling out his successor. So, as I was the one who always took the initiative, none of them had any cause to feel closer to me than the rest. Perhaps if I had indicated a preference. . . . But I was paralysed by the guilt of my survival, as certain they all resented my being alive as if I'd caused their comrade's death.

What can I do now? What am I to become? How can I live in this world I'm condemned to but can't endure? They couldn't stand it either, so they made a world of their own. Well, they have each other's company, and they are heroes, whereas I'm quite alone, and have none of the qualities essential to heroism—the spirit, the toughness, the dedication. I'm back where I was as a child, solitary, helpless, unwanted, frightened.

It's so lonely, so terribly lonely. I hate being always alone. I so badly need someone to talk to, someone to love. Nobody looks at me now, and I don't want them to; I don't want to be seen. I can't bear to look at myself in the glass. I keep away from people as much as I can. I know everyone is repelled and embarrassed by all these scars.

There is no kindness left. The world is a cruel place full of men I shall never know, whose indifference terrifies me. If once in a way I catch someone's eye, his glance is as cold as ice, eyes look past eyes like searchlights crossing, with no more humanity or communication. In freezing despair, I walk down the street, trying to attract to myself a suggestion of warmth by showing in my expression . . . something . . . or something. . . . And everybody walks past me, refusing to see or to lift a finger. No one cares, no one will help me. An abstract impenetrable indifference in a stranger's eye is all I ever see.

The world belongs to heartless people and to machines which can't give. Only the others, the heroes, know how to give. Out of their great generosity they gave me the truth, paid me the compliment of not lying to me. Not one of them ever told me life was worth living. They are the only people I've ever loved. I think only of them, and of how they are lost to me. How never again shall I sit beside someone who loves me while the world races past. Never again cross the tropic of Capricorn, or, under the arctic stars, in the blackness of firs and spruce, see the black glitter of ice in starlight, in the cold snow countries.

The world in which I was really alive consisted of hotel bedrooms and one man in a car. But that world was enormous and splendid, containing cities and continents, forests and seas and mountains, plants and animals, the Pole Star and the Southern Cross. The heroes who showed me how to live also showed me everything, everywhere in the world.

My present world is reduced to their remembered faces, which have gone for ever, which get further and further away. I don't feel alive any more. I see nothing at all of the outside world. There are no more oceans or mountains for me.

I don't look up now. I always try not to look at the stars. I can't bear to see them, because the stars remind me of loving and of being loved.

The Mercedes

For some reason taxis are always scarce in my district. Late on a wet night, the few there were would certainly be engaged, if their drivers weren't already sitting comfortably at home in the warm. So I was worried about getting one for M, who'd looked in earlier in the evening on his way to visit a patient. He'd seemed quite happy talking about the wonderful big Mercedes he was going to buy as soon as he had enough money, and the wonderful time we were going to have driving about in it together—which was a semi-serious game we'd been playing for years. Then the clock had struck, and he had suddenly jumped up and said he must go at once, as if the patient couldn't survive another half-hour without him.

At this point the telephone rang, and it was his wife, sounding annoyed and worried because the patient had rung up to say M hadn't arrived, and she'd guessed he was with me. She said I ought not to have let him stay because he got tired so easily since his illness, and shouldn't be out so late. In fact, on such a filthy night, he shouldn't be out at all, and it would be my fault if he got ill again in consequence. When I asked if she wanted to speak to M, he shook his head violently at the other end of the room, refusing to be involved. I didn't blame him.

It was a relief when the receiver clicked down. The final orders were for him to go home at once, in a taxi, on no account must I let him walk.

'No taxi,' he said immediately, when I told him : and he went to the door for his overcoat. I only just managed to stop him by getting there first. I knew how he hated being frustrated by practical things, and trying to get taxis from my house was always frustrating, but I said he must have one tonight. Holding on to him with one hand so that he couldn't slip out, I pulled the curtain back with the other to show him the weather. I was surprised to see how much worse it had got while we'd been talking and taking no notice of it. Sleet was driving across the street, filling its whole width with a whitish blur, hiding the houses on the opposite side. The wind was booming and blowing a gale, exploding against the window as if it meant to burst into the room; the tree outside groaned and creaked and lashed the glass with its branches. It was evident, even to M, that walking was out of the question. He threw himself on to the sofa, and sat there limp, his legs stuck out straight in front of him, looking the picture of gloom, and muttering to himself :

'Even the weather's against me. . . . I can't let the patient down. . . .'

'Yvonne says you're not to worry about the patient but go straight home.'

Still he sat gloomily staring at his shoes, not answering me. After a while, he sighed and murmured, 'It can't be helped. . . .' which was one of his phrases. I always thought all his disasters and disappointments were in it, as well as his courage and everything else. He'd come to live in exile in this country after losing everything in his own, and had had a terrible time, one way and another.

I said, 'Now I'm going to get you a taxi,' trying to
sound cheerful as if rows of cabs were waiting to be
called to the house, although I knew it would be a near-
miracle if I got one. Crouching on the floor, far too
nervous to sit on a chair, I dialled the taxi rank and
prayed for an answer. There wasn't one, of course. So
I kept on dialling different ranks and numbers, getting
more and more anxious each time I heard the bell at the
other end ringing vacantly in the dark distance.

Behind my back, M kept muttering sadly, 'If only I
had my Mercedes. . . .' Obviously he was ill and tired,
and it struck me for the first time that he'd begun to look
old. I could hardly bear it. It seemed so awful that he,
who was such a brilliant doctor and so good to his
patients, couldn't afford even a cheap car to take him
to them in this ghastly winter, while they were all racing
round like maniacs on four wheels. There was nothing
on earth I could do about it—except will a taxi to come.
And still there was only that empty ringing, as remote and
indifferent as if it was coming from outer space. I was
concentrating so hard that I didn't hear him move. But
when I looked round he had gone, the door was wide
open, his overcoat gone from the hook. I shouted, 'Wait!
Come back!' dropped the telephone and dashed after
him.

Struggling into his coat as he went down, he was already
at the foot of the stairs, and before I could reach him
vanished into the street. A great gust of icy wind came
charging into the house when he opened the door, nearly
blowing me backwards. The light swung round and round
crazily, shadows went leaping in all directions, everything
was distorted. I don't know whether I jumped or fell down
the last few steps, but somehow I got outside. The wind

yelled at me, tore violently at my hair and clothes, doing its best to force me back indoors. I couldn't think with all that booming and tearing; and with sleet driving into my eyes I couldn't see either. Yet I was dimly aware of a strange large shape looming in front of me, impervious to the weather.

The storm ended abruptly. Quite suddenly the wind dropped, the sleet turned to a gentle rain, through which the street lights appeared, quietly shining. M and I were on the pavement together, and the mysterious shape revealed itself as an enormous car standing right in front of my door, as if it belonged there. It looked like an electronic car, brand new and gleaming like ebony, with long, low, graceful lines and slender thrusting glittering fins.

M, who was always fascinated by expensive cars, went up to examine it closer. I stood looking on. Now there wasn't a sound. After all the commotion of wind and sleet, the sudden stillness seemed queer to me, even slightly disturbing, though he didn't appear to notice. Except for ourselves the short street was deserted, and all the windows were dark. There was traffic in the main road at the foot of the hill, quite near us, but passing as if in a silent film. The rain had stopped altogether, leaving the street a black river, with the reflected lights swimming across to glitter much more brightly on the magnificent car.

'It's a Mercedes!' M exclaimed suddenly in a voice of triumph, as if he'd known all along.

I wasn't exactly surprised myself. But I was thinking more about him. He was smiling, his face was shining and gay in the light, he looked younger and happier than he had for years. How could I have imagined he was looking old? He called out, 'Come and look,' but I was too fascinated to move. It was so long since I'd seen that mischievous, gay, twinkling smile of his that I'd almost forgotten it. All at once, I saw that he'd opened the door of the car; or else the car itself had opened it. 'Come and look,' he repeated, smiling over his shoulder at me. So I went and looked inside the Mercedes with him. The ignition key was there in its place.

It certainly was a marvellous car, a real beauty. I touched the seat, which was covered in some soft precious stuff, mink perhaps, warm, luxurious, smooth as velvet. The instruments on the dashboard sparkled like jewels.

'Shall I get in?' M asked, glancing sideways at me with a brilliant smile. His face wore a look I'd forgotten entirely: an adventurous, young, sly, delighted, audacious look which seemed to belong to the dim past when I'd first known him. At this moment, its reappearance was bewildering, startling, it gave me a little shock; which I suppose was why I didn't see him actually get into the car. But there he was, sitting behind the wheel.

The door was still open. I could have followed him. There was nothing to stop me getting in and sitting beside him. Why did I hesitate? Why was I so terribly nervous? I thought, Suppose the owner suddenly comes and finds us? but knew this wasn't the real reason.

'He won't,' M said, reading my thought. 'He's already here. *I'm* the owner.' I didn't feel like smiling, but smiled because he was joking. But was it a joke? Somehow it hardly seemed so. He looked so right, so at home, in the driver's seat, as if that was his proper place. Still without quite knowing why, I was starting to feel really frightened. If only he'd get out of the car and stand on the pavement with me . . . if only I could just touch him. . . .

He didn't move. Everything was so quiet, as if the silence was listening. Down in the main road, night traffic kept passing as usual, in full view, but without a sound. My little street held its breath, the houses stood watching, attentive to us. I turned my head quickly, and caught the one opposite which has a cross on the roof in the act of moving forward to see us better.

I'd only looked away for a second, but when I turned back to the car the door was shut and I couldn't see M properly any more. At once I felt terrified, seized the handle, tugged and wrenched it with all my strength, twisted it frantically from side to side. Nothing happened.

'Open the door! Do get out . . . please. . . . Don't sit there any longer, for heaven's sake! It's not our Mercedes. . . . You simply must get out!' Pounding the door with my fists in a panic, I hardly knew what I was saying.

The door didn't open. But now I could see M again quite clearly. He was looking at me through the window and smiling. The glass must have shut off his voice, I only just heard him say, 'It can't be helped. . . .' The words seemed to come from somewhere a long way off.

Suddenly, to my horror, the car started to move. I sprang at the door again wildly, determined to open it and get in, or else drag him out. Too late. The Mercedes was far out of reach already, my hands only grasped the air. 'Stop!' I shouted in desperation. 'You can't leave me behind!' All these years he'd been saying we'd drive off together, I simply couldn't believe he would go without me. Like a lunatic, I started running, while all the time the car was gliding away from me faster and faster, as smoothly and silently as water flowing downhill, and just as inevitably. Nothing I could do could possibly stop it; but still I rushed on in pursuit. There wasn't a sign or a sound from inside it. The street lights fled past like small moons, the houses swung round to watch. Tripping over uneven paving, splashing through puddles, I didn't look where I was putting my feet, but kept my eyes fixed on the back of the receding car until it reached the main road, where it disappeared instantly among all the others.

I stopped then. What could be more futile than chasing a high-powered car in a street full of speeding traffic? I couldn't have gone on running, in any case—I had no more breath. Besides, by now I knew it was useless. All my efforts, all my telephoning for taxis, had been for nothing, since M had abandoned me in the end. I knew there was no hope of ever seeing him again. Hadn't we always said we would never come back?

C

Clarita

It was terribly hot. I was lying naked on the top of the bed, feeling sweaty and itchy and trying to sleep. I felt as if I hadn't slept for a week.

Clarita came in from the veranda and stood just inside the room, looking at me, while I stared at her. I hadn't had time yet to get used to her beauty. She was so beautiful it made you gasp. Such grace. Slim long legs, tiny waist, heart-shaped face with enormous brown velvet eyes. And on top of all this some strangeness I can't describe, something almost frightening, so that I was half-frightened of her. But at the same time fascinated, absolutely.

She was humming a tune called *How You Look*. Then she suddenly stopped humming and said. 'What a sight—just look at yourself, will you?'

I did. A disgusting rash had spread all over me, I was covered from head to foot in red lumps and weals. There was lots of blood too where I'd been scratching. The itching was frightful, I simply had to scratch, or be driven mad.

'Stop it!' Her voice sounded cold, reprimanding, like a sadistic schoolmistress. 'If you go on scratching I shall tie your hands.' She sounded as if she would, too. She sounded as if she'd enjoy doing that. 'You disgust me,' she said, 'I've never seen anything so revolting. And suppose it's catching?'

She turned and walked out then and went into the bathroom next door. Through the thin wall I heard her run the water for a very long time, scrubbing her hands thoroughly, although she hadn't been anywhere near the bed, much less touched me. I knew she wanted me to hear the splashing because she meant me to feel unclean.

When she'd finished, I went and had a cold shower and washed the blood off. I thought the water might stop the itching, but it didn't. I thought of getting dressed and going outside, as it was dark now and might be cooler on the veranda. But then I lay down again on the top of the messed-up bed. Outside Clarita put on the record of *How You Look*.

Something sharp stuck into me when I moved. It was a small, hard, pink, polished, triangular thing with a sharp point, about a quarter of an inch long and about the same width at the base. Several others of different sizes were scattered over the bed. I searched round, felt in the folds of the sheet, discovered ten altogether, and laid them out in a row on the edge of the mattress. When Ktut passed the door I called him in and asked if he knew what they were. He jumped back as soon as he saw them, rolling his eyes until only the whites were showing. His teeth began to chatter so loudly it sounded like hailstones hitting the roof.

'Very strong magic,' he mumbled, 'Very *bad* magic,' and fled.

Torquil was talking to Clarita on the veranda. He was standing beside her chair, bending over her. Of course he must have been pawing her. Perhaps she'd just stopped him, who knows, perhaps she'd hit him, there was no sign of it. Now of course he stepped back.

The only light out there came through the lighted windows of the house and they weren't very bright. You couldn't have a light on the veranda because of the insects, etc. The floor was a pale indistinct stream, full of crocodiles and piranhas, on which we were floating, the chairs grouped round the table, a little boat. The jungle was right on top of us, just beyond the railing, a tremendous black menacing wall terrifyingly solid. The trees were almost close enough to touch. I was oppressed by that ominous great tree wall, all the time imperceptibly creeping closer to us, closing in. I looked away from it to the others, who seemed quite unperturbed. I wondered whether they realized. . . .

Clarita had her back to the windows, only one hand on the chair caught the light. Her hands were as beautiful as the rest of her, with smooth tapering fingers ending in perfect nails which she always kept beautifully lacquered and very long, almost as long as the gold artificial nails of the dancing girls. I suppose I noticed them specially because mine were ugly. My hands looked dirty no matter how hard I scrubbed them, my fingers were thick and stumpy, the nails ragged and bitten. I was so ashamed of my hands that I kept them hidden in my pockets as much as possible. Clarita said this drew people's attention to them.

It was the sort of thing she did say.

I was lying on top of the still unmade bed. I had to get some sleep somehow. I was dead tired, but the rash kept

me awake. At last I dozed for a few minutes. Then I was
awake again, scratching. All the triangles had somehow
collected in the folds of the sheet crumpled under me. They
were pricking me with their points, and one had em-
bedded itself in my thigh. The itching was intolerable
by the time I'd extracted it, the sheet was burning my
back.

I rolled off the bed, and standing there naked, thoroughly scratched my arms and armpits, my navel, my
shins. I must have done some pretty thorough scratching
before this, while I was half-asleep, judging by the amount
of blood. I was surprised my blunt fingers could produce
those long, deep, bleeding furrows, which looked more as
if they'd been inflicted by claws. Blood was running down
my shins on to the floor and there was blood on the
mattress as well as the sheet.

Clarita appeared, in a long gold dress made of some soft
silky stuff with a lustrous sheen and little ripples all
over it, like calm water reflecting a sunset and ruffled
by a light breeze. I could only think how lovely she
looked. She must have said something I didn't hear, because she was gesturing with her hands and the nails
flashed in the light. The next thing was that somehow my
arm was around her, I was clasping her tight with one
hand, while the other hand went on scratching until it
hurt, and really I couldn't tell whether her hand or mine
was tearing the flesh as I hugged her. I can't explain it.
Then she pushed me so hard that I nearly fell over. I
thought her beautiful dress must be covered in blood, but
there wasn't a spot on it anywhere. That frightening look
she had sometimes was on her face, I knew she was furious
with me without listening to what she said.

'Why can't you be a little bit kind to me?' I asked, almost ready to cry suddenly. 'Why is it you always want to hurt me?'

I picked up some of the triangles on the bed, and held them out to her on the palm of my hand. She looked at them in a puzzled way, saying, 'What on earth? Where?' and then she suddenly burst out laughing, and went on laughing so much she couldn't speak properly.

'I threw them in the waste-paper basket,' she gasped finally, still laughing.

And then I couldn't make up my mind whether she still looked frightening or not.

People were arriving, I heard cars outside. I had a look through the veranda door, but didn't want to show myself and asked Clarita what was happening.

I hadn't understood the situation, apparently. She was waiting to go out with this tall, good-looking young man who came in, wearing a smart uniform. I recognized D–B, and he certainly looked a dream-boat in that uniform. He looked as though he was modelling it.

'I'm taking her to dance at Lim's,' he told me. 'The dancing goes on all night, she can sleep at my place.' He was so pleased with himself and the gear and the way he'd arranged it. I thought the whole thing was in bloody bad taste. I tried to look at Clarita calmly to see whether she agreed to the plan.

'Expect me when you see me,' she said, going out with him. He said they'd be leaving at once in his car. I felt utterly wretched, abandoned, I could have burst into tears.

I heard a glass break. The crowd outside was making a lot of noise, you could tell lots of people were drinking.

I wished they'd all go away and let me get to sleep, there was nothing else for me to do. They started to sing *How You Look,* and I thought, now it's going to begin all over again. I thought I might as well get drunk with them out there, as I'd never be able to sleep through the row they were making.

I was driving this old racing Bug like a lunatic, chasing after Clarita, because I had to get her away from D–B. The idea obsessed me, I drove faster and faster, although the ghastly jungle road was no more than a track with holes in it four feet deep. It got narrower, worse, all the time. The trees came closer and closer, some with roots arching out of the ground as high as cathedral doors. Mysterious invisible creatures moved and moaned in the secret depths of the jungle. The headlights caught the lianas beside the road, bleaching them dead white, and they turned out to be huge white snakes, not lianas at all.

A giant python was hanging right over the road, sway-ing gently from side to side. I swerved, but there wasn't room to avoid it, in a flash it had slung one of its coils round me, immensely strong, and was pulling me out of the car. All I could do was cling on to the steering-wheel, I wouldn't let go of it, the python wouldn't let go of me, the Bugatti rocked crazily backwards and forwards. Then, at the last moment, the top of the windscreen somehow sliced off the whole loop of snake, and I drove on, all covered in snake-blood.

'I don't care a damn,' I called out, I don't know why, to Ktut who was watching from a flame-of-the-forest tree. His head and face were split down the middle, and orchids grew out of the crack—white ones. Their roots must have been somewhere behind the nose, as the flowers were coming out of the top of his head. His mouth didn't answer, it was probably full of roots like the throat, sinuses and other cavities, so that speech was impossible. The exhaust pipe fell off with a terrible clatter just then, the Bug crashed into the flame-of-the-forest tree, and I found I was a helicopter and went straight up in the air.

I saw a house in front of me. All the doors and windows were open, so I went in. There were no lights inside, it was completely dark, a thudding noise of drums spiked with electric guitars coming from somewhere. The heat was terrific. The air was thick and heavy and sweet with smoke, the floor packed with smokers, whose faces appeared momentarily when they took a puff. A voice said, 'Want to turn on?' and I asked for a drink instead, because I thought it would be quicker. I was afraid of losing Clarita for good if I didn't find her soon. The voice said, 'Everyone's blowing pot,' losing interest, and lost itself in the dark.

I'd been looking at all the faces in turn, scrutinizing each one at the brief instant of its illumination. But none of them belonged to Clarita, or to anybody I knew; they were all the faces of strangers. It made me sad. I had to get out of the place quickly, but I couldn't find the door. I felt my way along a wall, stumbling over people, asking them if they'd seen her. Nobody answered, and probably the question was not intelligible, as my voice sounded queer even to me, as if it wasn't my own.

The lights came on unexpectedly, and at once the heat became ten times worse. Every light radiated heat, and the masses of people, packed as tight as sardines,

generated more heat with their sweating bodies. They
overflowed out of the crowded rooms into the compound,
and even got into the jungle. I could see them because
strings of fairy lights had been tied to the sinister looking trees, making them look still more sinister. I saw the
snakes too, white, wreathed in white orchids, undulating
among them to a reptilian rhythm. The people were
laughing and talking at the tops of their voices there in the
jungle, oblivious of the snakes. They seemed not to see when
the savage streamlined shape of a leopard or a jaguar
stealthily parted the undergrowth just beside them, as
smoothly as a comb. The wild beasts looked peculiar
among all the humans, they looked almost as if they were
dancing, with the dim glimmery light flickering over their
fierce camouflage. From time to time one of them would
crouch flat on the ground, tense, the tip of its tail twitching, its muscles bunched for the spring, and then it would
pounce on some plump appetizing girl and drag her off in
its jaws. If she screamed there was too much noise to
hear, and no one seemed to notice these depredations.

So many bodies were pressed against mine that I couldn't
move, not even to scratch, though I was dying to. The
voices immediately around me seemed louder than the
rest, the din was frightful, I couldn't stand it. I felt nearly
out of my mind with the crowd, the heat, the noise and
the itching. Somehow I managed to cross my arms so
that I could scratch my left arm with my right hand, and
vice versa; but it was only a slight temporary relief. I
kept looking desperately from one face to another, all had
their mouths wide open, some full of half-masticated food,
some full of someone's tongue. Every mouth and every
face was a stranger's. In all that seething mob there
wasn't a single person I'd ever seen before in my life,

no one took the least notice of me. It made me feel horribly sad, for some reason.

Then I saw Torquil's face in the crowd, quite a distance away, and at least it was familiar. His mouth was screwed up, shouting, he waved his hands about as if he had something urgent to tell me. Naturally I assumed it was about Clarita, and shouted that I couldn't hear, we should have to come closer to one another. But with all the noise we couldn't understand what we were shouting, our voices got lost in the general uproar. I dived into the solid mass of steaming bodies, but couldn't fight my way through to him, though I still heard him shouting without making out the words. 'Where is she?' I shouted back frantically through that sea of noise. But now I could no longer hear him, I was right down on the sea-bed and knew he couldn't hear me, and by the time I'd struggled up to the surface again he had vanished from sight.

I was still looking about for him when someone bumped into me, and it was D–B who planted himself in front of me, deliberately blocking my way. He was much bigger than I was, I couldn't see or get past while he stayed there. He kept taking swigs out of a big bottle he held in one hand, and between the swigs he was shouting or singing, or perhaps laughing like a hyena—anyhow pouring out floods of atrocious noise; I was almost deafened.

'Shut up! Move!' I yelled at him, trying to kick his shins. 'What have you done with the girl?' I yelled again and again. But he only laughed that hideous hyena laugh of his without answering, tilting the bottle up and his head back. I watched the stuff gurgling down his throat. Then he had drunk the lot, the bottle was empty, and, wham, he bashed it down on my head, smashing it and my skull together so that I fell on the ground, and bits of

broken glass and bone flew through the air in all directions
as if they'd suddenly grown wings.

Then Clarita was there in her gold dress, close beside
me, smiling, and stretching out her hand as if she was
going to help me get up. I was delighted of course because she was so friendly. But she didn't speak or give
me her hand or do anything at all. And as I watched
her in the odd wavering light, she seemed to change, her
face looked different, the smile looked a bit mad, so
that I was almost frightened. My eyes were hurting, I
couldn't see properly, and this might have been why I
hardly recognized her any more and got really frightened.

Then she suddenly sprang at me and hugged me so
violently I felt shattered inside as if all my ribs were
broken. I couldn't move, I was paralysed. And now she
really did seem quite mad, and yet almost loving at the
same time, punching me in the face with her fists, and all
over. I didn't even want to struggle. Then she began twisting my arms and pinching my muscles, and ended by
crunching the bones of my hand together until I shouted
with pain, and to make her stop. But nothing could stop
her once she had tasted blood, she was clawing my hand
and wrist to the bone and licking the blood, then licking
my blood off her hand, and it was a tiger's paw, all
fierce and furry.

Out and Away

The umpire called, 'Out!' but it was not out. I saw distinctly that the ball was inside the line, and said so. There was no doubt about it. I'd dashed up to play at the net, I was nearer and better placed to see than she was; but she still persisted in saying it had been out. 'No arguing! You know the umpire's decision is final.' This was our form mistress who had it in for me left, right and centre.

'But the umpire's wrong—I know she is—definitely!' I was quite positive I'd seen correctly. My eyes were far better than hers, I was ten times quicker at seeing things. She wasn't really fit to umpire at all. I knew she couldn't follow the ball in a fast rally.

The form mistress again, 'That's more than enough from you. One more word and you stop playing.'

I protested, 'It isn't fair, that point was mine. . . .' but was interrupted.

'You heard what I just said. Leave the court at once and go in to your classroom.'

'Oh, all right, then,' I muttered to myself. '*Be* mean and unfair if you like—you don't know how to be anything else!' I was in such a rage that I hurled my racket down on the ground as hard as I could, and marched off without

76

looking at anybody.

'That girl's maladjusted,' I heard the umpire say as I passed. The word was popular with the staff that term. And I thought, maladjusted to what, for heaven's sake? To their stupid hateful school? I certainly hope I am.

I simply detested the place, loathed everything about it : the girls, the mistresses, the rules, the hideous uniform. I'd have run away if I'd had any money or anywhere to run to. I'd thought about getting a job as a cleaner or a waitress or something, but knew I didn't look old enough. No one would ever believe I was more than twelve, and sometimes I didn't even look that.

I went on being furious about the incident on the tennis court. The frame of my racket was badly bent, three strings had broken, and I couldn't afford to have it mended. Probably I could have borrowed the cash from the Games Club, as I was to play in the junior tournament, but that would have meant being lectured and told it was my own fault, and going over the thing about umpires again. Besides, I didn't want to play in the beastly tournament now. So I went to the noticeboard and crossed my name off the list. Whenever anyone said anything to me about it, I just told them I wasn't playing any more tennis, and then shut up like a clam. They couldn't get another word out of me, and went off looking annoyed and puzzled.

I felt I'd scored a slight success over this, so I decided in future not to speak to anybody at all about anything, except to answer direct questions as briefly as possible. It was rather fun, it made me feel superior to everyone else. I was surprised how easy it was not to talk once I got into the way of it. The girls in my form were most curious, they couldn't make out what I was up to : I think they thought I was playing some kind of secret trick on them. None of them believed I'd be able to keep up not talking. At first they tried to make me talk and join in things; not because they cared about me, simply to break my silence, which had begun to exasperate them. But after a few days, when they saw their efforts had no effect, they gave up and left me alone.

By this time I'd quite settled down to silence and solitude. Of course it wasn't complete silence as I had to answer questions and speak in class, and it's impossible ever to be alone in a school. But as far as I could I cut myself off and tried to behave as if the crowd round me didn't exist. I could tell how angry it made them by their behaviour. The girls in my dormitory thought they'd get their own back by sending me to Coventry, which was what I wanted, it suited me very well. Before long, more or less the whole school was ignoring me; I had no more trouble with people trying to make me talk. The staff paid very little attention to us. They lived separate lives, slept in a different house, and I don't think they noticed what was going on. Anyhow, they didn't appear to.

I was quite pleased with myself. Sundays were my only bad days. In summer we were supposed to spend fine Sunday afternoons out of doors, reading or writing letters. After the grass was cut in the paddocks it was left on the ground, and each Sunday pairs or small groups of girls would pile it up to make separate enclosures, inside which they were shut away from sight with their special friend or friends. This was the only time when I'd have preferred not to be alone. The staff were off duty, we were left to our own devices for the whole long afternoon from two o'clock until supper time; and during all these hours there wasn't a soul to be seen, the place might have been deserted. Of course I knew the garden and paddocks and orchards were thick with girls (we weren't allowed to go outside the grounds), but they were all invisible, hidden behind the roughly circular walls of heaped up hay, or perched in the convenient branches of the great cedar trees, or lying in dozens of hiding-places in the dense shrubberies, or among the great clumps of rhododendrons at the back of the outdoor stage, or between currant and gooseberry bushes and raspberry canes in the kitchen garden.

It was quite impossible then, as a solitary figure wandering round, not to feel conspicuous and excluded. I didn't want to be with the others, but I couldn't help being aware of the unseen eyes watching me from every side. It was a problem to know where to go. If I moved into any secluded spot, I was practically certain to stumble into concealed onlookers, which was the last thing I wanted. On the other hand, I didn't want to stay out in the open for hours and hours, knowing I was being spied on and laughed at and spoken about contemptuously by my enemies, who, for this one afternoon a week, seemed to be in a stronger position than I was. On this one occasion I longed for somebody to talk to; then I'd be able to forget the watchers I couldn't see, and the whispering in the bushes after I'd passed.

Then I did have someone to talk to, and it was all right. My twin sister, whom I hadn't even thought about since I was nine or ten, suddenly came to keep me company, just as she used to when I was a little girl. I was delighted to see her again. She always had such good ideas.

The Sunday she first appeared happened to be extremely hot. We walked slowly through the sun-bleached garden, then lay on the hard brown lawn near the mulberry trees. But when she suggested going into the shade under the drooping branches, I told her we couldn't because spies were sure to be there.

'They're watching us all the time,' I explained. 'It doesn't matter now you're here. Before you came it was starting to get me down—I used to dread Sunday afternoons.'

'If they're everywhere in the garden, why don't we two stay indoors?' she said. 'It'll be cooler there. And we'll have all the rooms to ourselves.' It was the obvious thing to do. And yet I'd never thought of it, and most likely I never would have.

I didn't mind being at school so much now. In fact, it was hardly like being there at all. I stayed quite separate from school life, alone and not speaking, and very often I went right away. It was fun to think of ways of being more and more apart from everything that went on. In class I had to be like the others; but the work was so easy I could do it without my real self being there.

It was a new thing, the going away, and it's rather hard to explain. It was just that I seemed to go into a vagueness, like a room does if you look at it out of focus. I don't know how to put it except like that. It's difficult to say just what I mean. Perhaps it was a little like walking in your sleep, because I once caught a flying glimpse of myself, either coming back or going away, and my face had the blank absent sort of look a sleep-walker's has. Not that I'd ever seen one; but there were pictures. Presently other people began to notice it. When the girls noticed I wasn't really with them, they would shout at me and pinch me to make me come back. I knew they did this, so I must have heard and felt them, but it was happening in another room and didn't affect me. I wouldn't come back, and there was nothing they could do about it.

Next the staff started looking at me and asking questions. Sometimes I'd come out of the vagueness to see a grown-up face frowning at me, a pair of grown-up eyes watching me and pretending not to. Sometimes a mistress's voice would say angry or silly things. But as I was always near the top of the form, and no fault could be found with my class work, there was nothing they could do either.

I suppose they all got used to me in the end. For a long time nobody bothered me, everything went on and on in the same old way. The only change was that the Sunday spying became more active : girls took to following us about, hiding in corners and trying to hear what my sister and I were saying. We didn't care. They didn't matter to us in the slightest, we hardly saw them. It was easy to ignore their stupid giggling.

I don't remember exactly when or why I was taken to see this psychiatrist. He seemed a nice friendly man, the sort you can talk to; so I told him about being maladjusted, and that I preferred it to being like everyone else at the school. I had the impression that he agreed with me. He didn't say much, but what he did say was sensible and understanding.

I didn't mind telling him things.

'This business about your twin sister,' he said. 'It's just a game you play, isn't it? Because you know you haven't got a real sister and never did have one.'

'You can put it like that if you want to,' I answered.

He smiled. 'How would you put it?' I told him I'd got out of the way of putting things in any way at all. He didn't press the point; he was a kind sort of man.

'And this going away,' he said to me at another interview. 'Can you describe it a bit more? Where do you go? What do you do there? Is it something like dreaming?' I thought hard how to tell him, I really tried. It was so simple, and yet so hard to put into words.

'Well, no, not really; it's more like this. . . .' When I started talking sentences came in a rush—'A person's either here or they're not here, aren't they? And if they're not here they have to be somewhere else, which means they must have gone away. . . .' I knew I hadn't made it any clearer, I'd confused things more. But he passed it over, and went on to ask:

'Why do you go away, do you think? Is it because you dislike being where you are?'

'Yes, for one thing. But that's only part of it. There must be something more, something stronger than that. Because lots of people don't like where they are, and if that was enough reason for going away a lot more people would be doing it, wouldn't they?'

I wondered whether it sounded absolute rubbish to him. I hoped he'd let it go, because I wasn't at all clear in my own thoughts just then. In a moment, everything began to dissolve in vagueness, except my voice which I could hear saying: 'It seems to me a person goes away because he or she has to make room for somebody else. It might be a case of two people sharing the same body, mightn't it? For instance, my twin sister might be sharing mine with me. In that case I'd have to go away whenever she came, wouldn't I?' She was really the one who said this, starting to speak with my mouth. I felt it go stiff as the last words came out, and my whole face set in that blank sleep-walking look as if I really was somewhere else. I was glad she'd come.

Now she could talk to him and explain about us and

make everything clear. She was always cleverer than I was. I felt relieved because now I could go away and didn't have to think any more.

Now and Then

Now it's sometimes difficult to believe he's the painter I first met four years ago.

Then he was completely absorbed in his work. He'd had important one-man shows in Paris and Amsterdam, his pictures were exhibited in galleries everywhere, all the critics agreed he had a brilliant future before him. Besides working hard, he did strenuous things when he wasn't working, liked climbing, swimming, speedboats, fast cars, was learning to fly his own plane.

Now he doesn't work at all any more. He's given up painting and all his other pursuits. Now the only thing he likes is to lie on a bed or a sofa, doing absolutely nothing.

Then he was very particular about his appearance, fastidious. He had eighteen pairs of shoes and a fantastic number of elegant suits for all sorts of occasions and climates. His shirts, which he sometimes changed several times a day, were specially made by hand, with an embroidered monogram on the pocket. I don't mean that he dressed formally. In the country, he often wore the same sort of clothes as the local people, only his were always made by a famous tailor and never lost their style.

Now he lounges about all day in a dressing-gown,

untidy, unshaved. When he does dress, his expensive clothes look as if they had been passed on by someone else, too tight for him, unpressed, stained with food, drink, ash, God knows what.

The first time I went out with him, I remember he wore a blue shirt and corduroy trousers as soft and as white as milk. He was very attractive then, very sexy. He wasn't exactly slim, but certainly not at all heavy, just muscular and solidly well-proportioned in the brown masculine Mediterranean way, with an aquiline profile and beautiful sea-coloured eyes set in long, long lashes.

Now he's put on weight and it doesn't suit him. It makes him look middle-aged, mediocre. His skin is still brown, but somehow it looks unhealthy, more like jaundice than sun-tan.

Outwardly, and in every other way, he's become totally unlike the man I married.

Then we had such a lot in common. Now we're absolute opposites in almost everything. Then he was lively, friendly, amusing; sociable, but able to do without people. His work always came first. Now he's become more gregarious since he stopped working, but in a disagreeable way. Every night he has to find somebody to drink with; he doesn't seem to care who it is.

Then, underlying his gaiety, there was a sort of secret seriousness, not displayed to the world, which to me was attractive, endearing. I could sense how seriously he was involved, with his work, and with all kinds of private, interior things. So I thought then, anyhow.

Now this inner seriousness has ceased to exist. His whole personality is entirely different.

Then he was quite content to be alone with me and his work. Now he has no time either for work or for me, but

only for strangers he picks up in bars. I simply don't
understand it.

We were alone together for two years, driving through
all the countries of Europe, staying wherever we felt
inclined. If only we could have gone on living like that.
It was perfect for me, I was perfectly happy. And I'm
sure he was happy too—I can't be wrong about that. We
were in love then, we had such close contact, he seemed to
share all my thoughts and feelings. He knew all my faults
too, all the bad things about me, and because he still
went on loving me, my guilt was wiped out. Now it has
all come back, and I feel guiltier than before.

Then we used to talk all the time, about anything, everything, talking nonsense lots of the time. We were never
bored for a single second. I remember pitying those
couples you see sometimes in restaurants, sitting silently,
glumly facing each other across a table, not speaking a
word. I was sorry for them then, and I despised them at
the same time.

Now we are like that. It seems incredible, but it's true.
He has nothing to say to me now, so that I can't talk to
him either. He hardly opens his mouth when we're alone,
seems to have no use for me except sexually.

It's all completely beyond me. I've never understood
why he stopped loving me and being happy with me.

Then I found him so attractive. Now he repels me
physically. I don't look at him if I can help it, because it's
only when he goes out drinking that he takes the trouble
to wash and shave. I can hardly recognize that stout,
grubby, dishevelled person sprawling on the couch as
the man I fell in love with almost at first sight.

It was four years ago, I admit. But can four years make
so much difference? Is it possible to turn into somebody

else in only four years?

We both happened to be staying at the same hotel. I remember I looked out of the window and saw him strolling off with a sketchbook under his arm. I had danced with him twice the night before. We hadn't talked much then. But, at that moment, when I looked at him through the window, it suddenly seemed vital to talk to him again, to hang on to him at all costs, not to lose him in life. Suddenly it was the most urgent thing in the world— if I didn't hurry he would elude me, disappear in the immense universe, and I'd never find him again.

I don't think I usually acted on impulse, even then; but I remember how I hurled myself into the lift and out of the place, and ran madly all through the hotel grounds, afraid he'd vanish once he got outside. Normally I'd have been afraid of being rebuffed or disappointed or something : but the compulsion I felt then was stronger than all those fears. I remember my tremendous relief when I caught up with him. I was much too out of breath from running to say a word and could only smile, but in what seemed a special new way, as if my whole self was smiling at him. I didn't have time to wonder if he'd be pleased to see me, because he immediately showed that he was.

It was all perfectly easy and natural, we might have been friends for years. The meeting might have been planned. We followed a lonely path, away from the sea and away from people, towards the silvery-blue mountain range. Occasionally we paused while he climbed a tree and came back with a handful of figs, warm and sugary from the sun, or stood making a pencil note in lines of fabulous economy and precision.

We talked about ourselves, naturally. I remember talking faster than usual, wanting him to know instantly and entirely all there was to be known about me. As we talked, I began to feel gay and alive, as I'd felt with those boys long ago who used to take me out on the backs of their motor-bikes. There was the same sense of easy contact and understanding, and of being someone of importance because I was liked, which had brought me to life in those days. At last, at last, it had happened again, and I was really living, instead of being a sort of no-person, merely waiting for life to start.

I remember that he too seemed elated, and that, for no reason but happy excitement, we ran down a grass slope to a dry river-bed full of big white stones, one of which I tripped over. He caught me as I was falling and kept his arms round me and his hands on my breasts. He wanted to make love to me there and then, and I said, 'Hurry up, before I change my mind,' and we lay on the hard warm ground with the tall silvery sun-dried grass rustling over our heads and the whole great blue dazzling arch of the sky behind.

I remember holding on to him tightly, not wanting to let him go, because I somehow felt it would never be quite the same again. Later, as we wandered back slowly without meeting a soul, it seemed to me more like a dream than something that was really happening. I suppose I couldn't quite believe in such happiness.

Perhaps I had no right to it. Anyway, it's gone now. My happiness has once more become a dream, and now seems never to have been real. Was it my fault that it vanished? I knew our marriage was a mistake, but I wasn't responsible, I was always against it. It was his father who kept on saying we ought to get married. Not that he liked me, he was barely civil. But I had some money and the prospect of inheriting more, and he wanted his son to have it, so we had to marry—that seemed to be how his mind worked.

I wanted to stay as we were. Why change things when we'd been living together so happily for over two years? I'd been prejudiced against the married state by my first experience. And Oblomov (but of course I hadn't started calling him Oblomov then) had been divorced recently, and his ex-wife wouldn't allow him to see their child. So we'd both tried marriage without success, and I saw no reason why we should try it again.

I expected him to agree with me. But now he too started saying we must get married. I put it down to his father's influence. But then a different motive emerged.

His first marriage was one of the few things we hadn't discussed in detail. I only knew vaguely that he was distressed about losing touch with his son. Now, to my amazement, it appeared that he wanted me to produce a child for him after we were married.

This gave me a severe shock. He'd always understood me so well, as if he really knew all I thought and felt. It was incredible that he shouldn't know how I loathed the whole disgusting business of reproduction. Even to think about it made me feel slightly sick. However, I was in love with him; I don't suppose I could have said no to anything he wanted me to do then. So, as marriage was what he wanted, I went through with it, though not without considerable misgiving.

I was thankful to get it over. And still more thankful when his father went off and left us alone again. I couldn't wait to get back to our former happy existence of intimacy and seclusion. I might have known that it wouldn't happen like that.

It was just as if we hadn't really got rid of the old man, he might still have been with us, surrounding and enveloping us with his influence wherever we went. He was always coming into the conversation, always coming between us.

It was then that Oblomov began to change into Oblomov, and I first began thinking of him by that name. Quite quickly, he seemed to lose interest in his work and everything else, spent fewer and fewer hours painting and more and more doing nothing at all.

At the same time, he developed a guilt complex because his father had accused him of being neglectful during the period when he and I had been so happy together. He didn't tell me this, but I didn't need to be told. The father's astral body was always floating about, revolving around us both. It was worse than having him there in the flesh.

I half expected to find him waiting for us each time we moved. And he really did materialize for me almost physically whenever we arrived at a fresh hotel, appearing in some prominent place where I was bound to see him, posing on the stairs very often showing off his cummerbund and his neat waist line, and smoking a thin black cigar. For a change now and then, we would rent a villa for a short time. Then I used to dread going into the house, knowing he'd be there first, spreading out his belongings in the best room, and would immediately confront me with demands for wood fires and unobtainable things to eat. All this had a more devastating effect on me than his actual presence.

While this apparition invaded my life, I had to watch the serious painter, the ardent, dynamic man who had seemed like a part of myself, growing always more lethargic, indifferent, inaccessible, lying about all day in a dressing-gown and going out drinking at night, as Oblomov replaced him in front of my eyes. The change was all the more horrible to watch because I had absolutely no understanding of what was happening. I kept imploring him to discuss the situation with me, but he always refused. In fact, he soon seemed not to want to talk to me about anything.

I tried and tried to persuade him to start work again. As he wouldn't get up, I used to bring his sketchbook and leave it with the charcoal beside him, hoping he would do some drawing while I was out of the room. But later, when I came back, I always found the things exactly as I'd put them down.

I tried in every way I could think of to distract and amuse him, but he only seemed irritated by these attempts. I knew I hadn't changed, I was just the same as I always had been : but eventually I was forced to see and admit that he no longer liked being with me, or wanted to do the same things as I did.

My nature is energetic, it's impossible for me to do nothing, I must always be occupied. So I rushed around doing any number of quite unnecessary things, simply to kill time.

Since he knew all about me, he must have known I couldn't help being full of energy. Yet he seemed to resent my activity, very much as I resented his idleness. He took it as a reproach. I didn't mean it like that (not consciously, anyhow), although his prolonged refusal to make the least effort had begun to get on my nerves. I was exasperated at times by his perpetual loafing, by seeing him limp and inactive, still not even properly dressed, late in the afternoon. And once I remember snapping impatiently : 'You might at least tie your shoe laces before you trip over them.'

'I suppose, if I did, you'd accuse me of falling down drunk.'

I was startled by his reply. He'd never spoken to me like that before, his voice sounded so hostile, as if I was always accusing him, nagging him, about something; which was quite untrue. And he was looking at me in a way I didn't know either; so coldly and distantly, like a judge considering what punishment I deserved for my crimes.

Suddenly, for the first time for months, I felt guilty again; and afraid. I'd got so used to relying on his complete support. Now, suddenly, he'd withdrawn it—worse still, he was actually against me. How could it have happened? Were we really so far apart? Up to now, I seemed to have deluded myself into thinking of his diminished interest as no more than a temporary aberration that was bound to end soon. Only at this moment did I realize fully that things had changed fundamentally, and perhaps permanently, between us. There was no more contact, no communication. Unbelievably, he had changed from a lover who loved me in spite of my faults into a judge condemning me coldly, from far away.

In sudden panic, I apologized for what I'd just said, tried to explain that I'd spoken involuntarily and that the words had really been an expression of my own sadness, guilt, incomprehension—now indeed I was expressing all those complex emotions. He said nothing, didn't seem to be listening. He had ceased to be interested in my emotions, they no longer concerned him.

Now at last it was only too clear that I was about to lose him, if he wasn't already lost.

I was both terrified and incredulous. It didn't seem

possible that our relationship could have deteriorated to such an extent without my noticing; and yet, obviously, it was so. For weeks and months past I must have been blind, or mad. And now, in my confused agitation, I couldn't think straight and had no idea what to do.

At about this time, his father got ill and sent for him. We had to go. I half let myself hope that living a different sort of life in another country might eliminate Oblomov, and restore the real man as his true self. Needless to say, it has done no such thing.

Since we came to live here, he's only grown more lethargic than ever. Even an indirect reference to his work makes him flare up at once and shout at me to shut up and leave him alone. It's true that he drives over most days to sit with his father. But that's absolutely all. Apart from that, he does nothing whatsoever but laze and chain-smoke, scattering ash everywhere, until it's time for him to go out for his evening drink.

I remember the time when unintelligent people bored him. Then he used to say he'd rather talk to me than to anyone in the world. Now whole days often pass when we don't exchange more than two words. Yet every evening he goes to the pub, and stays there talking for hours. Now he only seems to like uninteresting talk with his inferiors. He enjoys stupid parties, gossip and dirty stories. It's as though he's deliberately lowered himself to the level of yokels and dull commuters without a thought in their heads. This transformation defeats me, I'm utterly baffled by it.

Nothing on earth would induce him to pull up a weed in the garden, or walk as far as the letterbox at the corner. But he'll willingly drive thirty miles to a cocktail party that's certain to be a most crashing bore, dragging me along with him, in spite of my protests.

He knows how I loathe these idiotic parties, how isolated and miserable I feel among dreary strangers with whom I have no point of contact, who don't even speak my language, and, judging by his expression, this pleases him. He seems to regard it as a punishment I deserve. (But why is he punishing me? What have I done?) After the first few moments, I'm always dying to get away. He knows this too, and that he can keep me waiting as long as he likes, as we have to drive home together, and he is often one of the last to leave. I can't imagine what satisfaction he gets out of talking such drivel all this time; unless he does it to spite me, or for the pleasure of slipping in his nasty little cutting remarks every now and then.

He's developed a vicious streak which he never had in the past. Then he was always good-natured, well-disposed towards people, polite and friendly. He would never have hurt anybody intentionally. Now he often says things that are really cruel : mean, sneering, horrible things; but always as if he's joking and doesn't mean what he says. I can only suppose these people are stupid enough to believe he is merely teasing, or surely they wouldn't invite him into their homes.

Now he loves to create awkward situations so that everybody's embarrassed. It's a mystery to me how he gets away with it. If the party is fairly formal and the other guests are all wearing conventional clothes, he'll turn up in a blue corduroy smoking-jacket bound with white satin braids, or a sequin-trimmed scarlet tunic with gold epaulettes. In conversation, he keeps using four-letter words all the time just to shock the person he's talking to. And he almost invariably drinks far too much. Yet, for some unknown reason, nobody seems to mind. He is tolerated, and apparently even liked.

Personally, I hate to see him showing off, knocking back glass after glass, being either outrageously flattering or wildly offensive, or else gazing with mock-soulfulness into the eyes of some dim-witted female who's too stupid to see that he's making a fool of her.

I don't know why I'm distressed by his rudeness when no one else cares. Especially as I can see that, in spite of it, he really is popular, as, when at last we are leaving, somebody so often asks us to go on to another house. Then, while I'm saying how late it is, trying to decline politely, he'll push me aside and drown my voice by exclaiming in loud, genial tones sounding completely false :

'Fine ! Of course we'll come. Of course it isn't too late. It's never too late for me—I never want to go home. Being at home is worse even than being out !' And because he evidently says this primarily to insult me, the silly fools don't seem to notice he's insulting them too.

Now I have the horrid duty of watching carefully, without letting him know it, to see if he's unsteady on his feet, or whether he's fit to drive. I don't suggest driving myself unless he's obviously incapable, because I know how angry it always makes him.

Four years ago he was always equable and good-tempered. Now he's absurdly touchy, flies into sudden rages over trifles, shouts abusively at me in front of people. What worries me more though is the fact that he seems to have stored up some obscure grudge against me, but refuses to say what it is.

Once we were so close that we almost seemed able to look into each other's minds. Now neither of us has any ideas what the other is thinking. If I remember his devotion and kindness and how happy he made me, I have the impression of thinking about someone else, an entirely different person who has died, or gone away for ever to some remote continent.

It's too painful to look at him now when I remember how attractive he used to be with his beautiful sea-green, sea-blue eyes, where I seemed to see, like a mysterious secret, that inner seriousness of which not a trace remains. Then his face was marvellously expressive, full of sensitivity, life, warmth, intelligence, interest. Now it's grown coarse, lost its vitality and its clean-cut lines; now it only expresses surliness, sloth or spite.

His muscular build has degenerated into fleshiness. The weight he's put on makes him look clumsy, almost bloated at times, almost gross.

His expensive eccentric clothes are always so creased and spotted I sometimes think he messes them up on purpose, that he's determined to look neglected. At all events, I can see no sign of his old fastidiousness. There's nothing left now that I can identify with the man I loved. He often seems more like a stranger, an enemy even, who has commandeered the house I live in, and whose presence is forced upon me.

Now I've almost begun to dread opening the door beyond which I know he will be lolling on the sofa. He's forbidden the cleaning woman to go in there, so the room's always dusty and in confusion, old newspapers and empty cigarette packets strewn all over the floor, bottles and dirty glasses left everywhere. A fog of stale smoke hangs visibly from wall to wall. Smoke has dulled the brilliant lustres to soupy brown. All the windows are shut, the thick smoke nearly chokes me, stings my eyes till they start watering.

He doesn't move when I come in, just lies there flat on his back, bulky, ungainly, inert, staring into space. Can this slack, sluggish, morose individual once have climbed trees and brought me ripe figs to eat? Now he doesn't look as if he could ever have climbed a tree in his life. Ash drops from the end of his cigarette, he blows a smoke ring without looking round, without giving me a glance.

Standing a little distance away from the sofa, I have to make an effort before I can speak to him. I ask if he wants any lunch. There's no answer. A cup of coffee? No reply. The paper? Silence. Well, then, shall I open a window a bit to let out the smoke? It's so thick in here one can hardly breathe. Still he says not a word, doesn't look, but negligently, as if I wasn't there, tips more ash into the folds of his dressing-gown. For a second I really wonder if he's the same man. . . .

Then suddenly I get angry. I hate this surly, ponderous layabout who won't answer me; this shirker who's sold out to lethargy and indifference, betraying his own potential. He's so gifted, he could be famous, he could do almost anything with his life; and he deliberately chooses to do nothing whatever—to waste it in indolent apathy. That's what is so utterly infuriating.

It enrages me, absolutely. I'm so furious I'd like to set fire to the sofa to make him move. I simply can't bear to see him lying there, torpid, supine, letting all his splendid abilities go down the drain. It's such a shame, such a terrible waste. It's wicked to throw away so much talent out of sheer laziness. It's such a damned shame it's a crime. I can't stand it—but what the hell else can I do?

Well, at least I need not stay in this room any longer. I don't have to go on looking at him. . . .

I rush out to the kitchen, and in rage and frustration,

D

with all my strength, I hurl cups and plates on to the tiled floor, where they're smashed to atoms. Then I stamp on the fragments, grind them to powder under my heels.

Then I feel ashamed of myself, find a brush and start sweeping up the mess.

High in the Mountains

It's simply not true, what he says, that it slows one's reactions. Of course some drugs do, but the exact opposite is true of this one, it actually makes people quicker and more accurate in their movements. The tennis professional who first gave it to me knew what he was doing. He told me I'd play a better and faster game afterwards, and I did; in fact I won the tournament. Yet just now Oblomov shouted at me, 'You're not to drive, Jane, while you're taking that stuff.'

I'd just reversed the car out of the garage and had my back to the house when he came to the door; so I pretended not to have seen or heard him, and roared away down the drive. Why does he keep watching me all the time, following me about? Has he been told to watch me? Who would tell him? Doctors? Police?

Ahead, the evening sky's clear after the storm, though the rest of it is still covered by black thunder clouds. The blue-green sweep in front looks cold and clean like deep water, and there's a fan of tawny light just above the horizon, which must be where the sun has set, no, it can't be, that's not the west. Perhaps it's a fire. It's a long way off, anyhow. I keep driving towards that point on the horizon, and at intervals it shoots out a long ray of light,

99

a lighthouse beam to guide me to the magic mountains where I'll be safe from all the horrors piled up behind me. Without looking round, I can feel the huge storm clouds towering up, black and menacing, smouldering at the edges, like the walls of hell.

Our house is somewhere in the shadow of those ominous clouds, they are waiting to fall on it, then the walls will collapse and crush me. That's why I'm driving so fast, to get away from the house, and from him, sitting inside like a spider in its web, waiting to pounce on me. I'll only be safe when I get to the mountains. I can see him sitting there smoking, waiting for me to come back, doing nothing except watch and wait. He never does anything else; that's why I call him Oblomov. Everything in the room watches: the clock watches, the pictures on the walls watch, the nudes roll their eyes each time the ash drops off the end of his cigarette, occasionally into an ashtray, but usually on to the carpet, or on to his clothes.

I can't bear to be shut in the house with him. Men are animals, beasts of prey, and I'm the prey he has caught. He's so pleased with himself, thinks he owns me, but really he's only a great heavy animal lying on me, crushing me until I can hardly breathe. He's altogether too massive for me, I can't stand his weight, his size. He eats too much, drinks too much, smokes too much: wears his fat like an expensive suit he's proud to be seen in. 'In ancient China,' he says, 'fat was considered the sign of a successful man.' I don't care about ancient China. To me it's just beastliness and a sign of his animal nature.

At least I shan't have to eat with him tonight, that's something. It almost makes me sick to watch him chewing and chewing, puts me right off my own food. He doesn't know that. If he happens to notice I'm not eating, he says the dope takes away appetite. He's always lecturing me on the evils of drug taking, watching to see when I take a shot, trying to stop me. It makes me furious, when he does far worse things himself; nauseating things that upset other people.

I think smoking and drinking are vices, disgusting habits, they're so offensive to everybody. The smell of stale smoke in our house is revolting, it clings to the curtains, the bedclothes, no matter how often they're washed. Smoke hangs inside the lampshades, turns the ceilings yellow. Then, when he drinks too much, he gets quarrelsome and aggressive, embarrasses people by stumbling about and making stupid remarks. What I do never affects anyone else. I don't behave in an embarrassing way. And a clean white powder is not repulsive; it looks pure, it glitters, the pure white crystals sparkle like snow.

How beautiful the snow is when it covers the ground, hiding all the mess and ugliness man has made under its calm austere white. I wish I lived in one of the cold countries where there's snow all the year. The high mountains are like archangels, aloof and lovely and awe-inspiring, standing above the earth with their glittering heads in the sky. I adore the high mountains, I could worship them. I dream of becoming identified with them, cold and inaccessible like their snow-covered summits. Something about their remote perfection makes me want to die.

I know I've got a death-wish. I've never enjoyed my life, I've never liked people. I love the mountains because they are the negation of life, indestructible, inhuman, untouchable, indifferent, as I want to be. Human beings are hateful; I loathe their ugly faces and messy emotions. I'd like to destroy them all. People have always been horrible to me; they've always rejected me and betrayed me. Not one of them has ever been kind. Not one single person has even attempted to understand me, to see things from my point of view. They've all been against me, ever since I can remember, even when I was six years old. What sort of human beings are these, who can be inhuman to a child of six? How can I help hating them all? Sometimes they disgust me so much that I feel I can't go on living among them—that I must escape from the loathsome creatures swarming like maggots all over the earth. In a desperate moment, I once said this to Oblomov, who was horrified, shocked, utterly unsympathetic. He looked at me as if I was a criminal, he almost shuddered. 'Don't say such things! If anyone heard you talking like that they'd think you were insane. I suppose you realize it's not normal. . . .' Is it normal to stifle me as he does, so that I have to rush out of the house before the walls close in and crush me completely? It's he who compels me to drive and drive, as I'm driving now, to save myself from suffocation and from all the people I really can't stand.

Switch on the headlights, it's getting dark. A sign ahead : X-ROADS. SLOW. Houses beyond the hedges. I hate this dull, flat country, all hedges and walls and fences; it's like an overcrowded prison. Or an enormous ant heap, teeming with millions of slaves, who can't think, but only obey, and who are so terrified of anything new or strange they have to live behind barricades. As long as Oblomov sits inside the walls of the house everything's under his control, but he's scared stiff outside. If he was with me now he'd be sweating and swearing. 'Over eighty —you're out of your mind!' I despise beyond words his considerate driver's caution, I can't bear to be driven by him. But he never lets me drive if he's in the car.

Driving alone in the dark is a bit like dreaming. I dream I'm leaving the awful world of people behind, going to the non-human world, to the snow and ice of the high mountains. If only I can get there . . . if only I can drive far enough, fast enough. . . . I must hurry, hurry. It's such a long way to the mountains, they're not even in sight. I'm still among built-up areas, far too much traffic, far too many people, delaying me, getting in my way—I could shoot them.

Thank heaven this old car's still fast. It's big and high-powered and passes everything on the road; I don't need to dream that. It's wonderful driving alone at night, driving fast, the headlights slicing a way for me through the darkness, everything racing towards me and then wiped out, obliterated. Nothing exists behind me.

There, beyond those trees, what's that light in the sky? Not the lighthouse beam now . . . not the fan. . . . A hair-thin sickle, a brand new moon, as thin as the finest thread. I'm looking at it through the windscreen, through glass, and that means bad luck. What on earth made me think of that old superstition? Poor moon, you've lost your old magic, you couldn't hurt anyone if you tried. You're not even mysterious any more. The rocket that fell on your virgin surface degraded you, put you into the clutches of human beings. Man always destroys magic and beauty wherever he goes, he contaminates everything. Only the highest mountain tops remain invincible in their frozen splendour.

Come on, old car, soon we shall see the mountains, the country's getting more open. You and I are good friends, I understand you, don't I? We both love speed. Fewer and fewer houses here. Soon we'll be on our own, as we were on those long trips when we drove away from the hot

crowded beaches, from the orange peel in the warm sand,
following the lonely roads northwards, just us two together
under the lonely moon, on and on, all night long, never
stopping, until the moon went down, the sun rose, and
the snows of the Alps caught fire.

No more walls or hedges, the mountains in sight at last.
At last we've got away from towns and traffic and road-
signs and dogs and people. We've overtaken all the cars
and the heavy lorries. Faster! . . . Faster! The way's
clear ahead. Now we can really start moving—that's
splendid, you're doing fine!

No more human beings, no more obstructions. Nothing
in front but the mountains, the climbing road, the wind
tearing at us, trees swishing past like ghosts. A continuous
stream of woods and boulders races away into darkness.
A board flashes by: ATTENTION! DANGER! CHUTES DE
PIERRES. Now the sound of water somewhere, a torrent
hurtling down into a black abyss leaves its watery chill
on my skin. Like an apparition, all of a sudden, a giant
cliff soars up, a spectral white wing gently unfolding above.
A kind of shiver goes through me. The first glimpse of snow
on the mountain top always brings this electric thrill.
Here is something man can never debase.

Snow peaks are standing all round the sky, phantom-
pale in the night, vast disembodied ghost-shapes, larger
than life, floating in luminous pallor, the moon's ethereal
crescent gliding between. Am I driving or dreaming?
Dreamlike, these colossal, fantastic mountains, aloof like
gods. Dreamlike sky-diving moon. Dream road, unending,
always spiralling upwards. Nightmare road, verging on
dizzy chasms, a knife-edge eternally twisting in steeper and
sharper bends. Shall I ever get round the next one? It's
so narrow, the curve is so violent, there's barely room. I

spin the wheel, and I've made it, time after anxious time :
and still the loops of the road unfurl, each turn harder
to negotiate than the last.

A sudden startling movement; round the next bend,
some large dark object approaching me on the road. A
car full of people, their faces blanched white by the headlights, which instantly jump aside as I wrench the steering-wheel round. People! But how is it possible? They
have no right to be here . . . their presence is a disaster,
an abomination. It means that the mountains are not
inviolate, after all; that there's no escape from people
anywhere in the world. Am I going to admit that, to let
them pass? No, no—destroy them! Something erupts inside
me, a hard excitement. Destroy them—don't let them
defile the white purity of the snow!

The headlights pounce again, the white flare of light,
jabbing forward, becomes a sharp instrument to impale,
to eviscerate. Four shapes are transfixed, four white faces,
frighteningly close, against a black backdrop of reeling
mountains, white fish-faces staring with open mouths. The
air goes colder and darker, thunder booms in the ice;
ice-cold breathing down from the summits like a com-
mand. Assert the supremacy of the high mountains. New
uncontrollable surge of excitement. Away with the in-
truders who dare to profane the heights! Out of my sight
with them, out of the world!

Dry scatter of flying pebbles, screeching tyres thin eerie
yelping sounds lost in the jar and jolt of collision; my big
car staggers and hesitates on the rim of black nothingness.
Out on the road, other wheels are moving, slowly,
smoothly, inevitably, over the edge of the precipice, first
the back wheels and then the front; accompanied by weird
high yelps, soon extinguished, the car disappears with its

occupants, deliberately, in slow motion. It seems a long time before the bottomless black swallows it.

There, it's gone now. Only tyre marks over the edge to show what has happened. The watching mountain tops stand round in their stupendous circle, impregnable and superb. I've done it. Triumphant, I press my foot down hard and drive on.

At last I feel identified with the mountains, clean, cold, hard, detached. I've cut myself off for ever from all mankind; the ugly pointless mess and muddle of human life no longer concerns me. Once and for all, I've declared myself against life and people, on the side of otherness and indifference, isolation, the mineral beauty of the non-human world.

The road unaccountably seems to have straightened out, no more hairpin bends. I look up from it to the mountains; but now I can't see them, they have withdrawn like phantoms into the pitch-black night. I keep looking up for them as I drive, but still never catch sight of the glimmer of snow. And yet, at the same time, I'm all the while standing somewhere a long way off, among the unmelting snows of the highest summits, and I'm as indifferent and aloof and as coldly invulnerable as they are. Except, perhaps, for the dim awareness, far out on the extreme periphery of perception and too remote to disturb me, of certain sequences of future events, which it will not be possible to avoid. . . .

Among the Lost Things

The new, the great, the divine star is like no other. It alone has the glory, the godlike power to create new forms of life and a world of its own. It came into being at the midwinter solstice, while man was celebrating the birth of a god.

Now the star is man's new god, producing changes unprecedented in his planetary environment, setting in motion undreamed of chains of events, destroying delicate balances which took millenniums to evolve.

How it glittered in meteoric flight, shooting up like a stupendous missile to its place in the sky. Its brilliance set the darkness on fire, its rays touched the earth with magic and laid their spell on the earth's inhabitants. The eardrum–bursting roar of its ascent heralded a new era beyond the reach of the human imagination.

Already its radiations have changed biological patterns, transmuted the immutable, evolved strange variations. Which of these variants, if any, ultimately become stable, is still in doubt. And whether the human race will survive in any recognizable form depends on the new god-star which is remaking man and the world.

In the sky, as on earth, all the power, all the glittering glory, belongs to the star. Its magnificence has dimmed the sun and put out the planet's eyes. It is a conflagration of splendour where nothing was.

Where am I? Who? . . . Can't be sure of anything since the star. . . . It's dark here and things keep changing. Nothing's ever the same for long.

I lose things all the time. In the dark. I don't drop or mislay them, I don't leave them behind. I just find they aren't there any more. Suddenly they've gone.

I don't understand all these changes. They began with the star. I'm changing myself. I can feel it. I shan't change back to what I used to be, I know that. It's the same with the lost things. They've gone for good. I'll never find them again. Basic essential things, always taken for granted, drift away and dissolve, get lost, change into totally different things. It's disturbing.

Darkness thickens, rises, creeps up to my knees. To my waist. Vertebrae collapse, spine sinks into the dark. Hair goes next. Face now. Eyes sucked out of sockets, smooth as oysters sliding down the black drain. Suddenly they're all among the lost things. The dark ingurgitates everything, myself included. It's disturbing all right.

The hands of the clock always at 5.15. Morning? Afternoon? Can't tell in the dark. Is it always the same room? No way of telling that either. Time and place are among the lost things. Sex as well. Male and female interchangeable now. Trans-sexualism they call it. It's because of the star.

Shadows thick on the walls, black in the corners. Sky must be black outside. I can't see it. There's a tree. It grows so close that branches touch the window. Leaves keep stirring slightly, continuously, soundlessly now. They bring messages sometimes. Did leaves always. . . . Now they're dark moths swarming against the glass.

Leaves begin moving differently, all at once. Flashes of brilliant silver, of blinding white light, glide between the branches. The light of the star. I don't want to see it. It must not touch me. I step back, away from the window, beyond its reach.

An obscure doubt skids over the back of my mind, makes me look down at myself. Sex apparently still female. I'm wearing a skirt, anyhow.

One of the other sex enters, cheerfully. 'Hullo there! All in the dark?'

'You know I like it.'

'O.K. I won't put on the light.'

I feel him lower his hand from the switch, feel relieved. Why doesn't he go now? He knows he shouldn't come in here. He only does it to make me anxious. I'm always tense, uneasy, while he's in the room. Especially now, when I can't really see him. Where exactly is he? What does he want? I know he enjoys my uneasiness, prolongs it deliberately. That's typical of him. He's spiteful.

Conversation seems to be what he wants at present. 'They were talking about us up there—about you. They didn't hear me coming. I stood in the passage and listened.'

'What did they say?' I don't care, don't want to know, but know that I have to ask.

'They said they wondered you weren't afraid to live alone with me here, in this lonely house.' His voice changes, it sounds different now. It sounds teasing, but in a malicious sort of way.

'Why should I be?'

'In case I did something to you.'

'What sort of thing?'

'Did you in.'

Teeth gleam faintly. A grin. He moves then with loose, swaggering strides I can't see, cowboy swing from the hips, thumbs hitched in low-slung belt. There's almost no light now. Even against the window he's only a vague dark shape, leaning forward slightly, staring at dark night, at nothing. His forehead must be touching the glass. Is he listening to the whispering of the moth-leaves? What mysterious information, secret orders, do they impart? Instantaneous silver, bright on his hair, gone again in a flash. Why isn't he afraid of the star?

'Are you frightened?' he asks chattily. 'Of being murdered, I mean.'

'I never thought about it.'

'Never?' Shadow face turns towards me. Again the faint gleam of teeth, which continue to show dim-white after voice has spoken. 'Perhaps you should, you know. Just to be prepared. Just in case. Because I might have to kill you, one of these days.'

'Why?'

The disembodied grin still hangs in the air. Murderer's grin? Cheshire Cat's?

'I might be forced to, don't you see? It might be the only thing I could do. That's the point.'

'I don't understand.'

'Don't you?' Silence. The total darkness makes the room a solid black cube. I can't see him at all now, not even against the window. He's moved. Unexpected from over there on the left, his voice startles. 'Well, think what's happening to you.'

'What on earth are you talking about?' Fear in my voice —has he heard it?

His voice, lazy, spitefully teasing, gives nothing away.

'Oh, come now. . . . Don't pretend not to understand when you know as well as I do. . . .'

'I tell you I don't! I haven't the slightest idea what you mean.' Without much success, I struggle to keep some control.

More silence follows. The deeply preoccupied mind, functioning in depth, is aware that he's moved again. Soundless moves in the dark have brought him close behind me. I feel him standing there threateningly, hand (hands?) uplifted. What's he going to do? A second of panic.

He strikes a match and reveals his position. Not behind me, after all, a bit to one side. The tiny flicker seems both momentary and ages long, makes the dark more menacing, more intense, afterwards. His face materializes intermittently as an indistinct blur whenever the cigarette is drawn upon, otherwise it remains invisible. I stare and stare, anxiously awaiting each reappearance. In between glimpses, I simply can't think what it's like, that face. I can never remember it. Queer, when I remember movements so well. The face never seems to be the same twice.

At last the voice speaks again. 'You know perfectly well how you're changing. That's why you shut yourself up here.' A pause comes after these profoundly disturbing words, during which terror slowly lifts its evil interior head. A few more words. 'You've only got to look in the glass.'

Another pause, while the black bud of horror slowly expands and flowers. 'You mean? . . .' My mouth is so dry I can hardly produce a whisper.

'Just what you think I mean.' The voice is cruelly casual, confident, firm.

Imagination proliferates suddenly like a malignant

growth. Nightmare monstrosities crowd the dark room.

'No, it couldn't possibly happen! Not to me. . . .' The words pour out at random, almost regardless of sense. 'Not to anyone biologically stabilized . . . a fully mature adult person. . . . What about D.N.A. . . . the genes and all that! . . .' The voice has the sound of desperation, of despairing appeal, as if addressing a judge whose verdict it can't be expected to influence. Perhaps the man I can't see is a judge. I don't know anything about him.

'The phenomenon is quite without precedent, the situation entirely new.' His voice, changed again, unlike the malicious tones I've been hearing, speaks with a certain judicial detachment, deliberation. 'We have no frames of reference. No knowledge of anything comparable. And so everything is possible.' Pause. Then, as if talking down to a child : 'Until just lately to change sex would have been considered impossible.'

'But this other thing really is impossible. . . . I just don't believe it. . . .' Can that voice be mine, speaking so wildly and childishly, almost with the sound of tears?

The cigarette is finished, is stubbed out. Unseen movements are sensed in the unlit room, this time towards the door. At last he seems to be going. The door handle clicks as it turns, the face turning with it. Again a pale gleam of teeth, then it's gone.

With my eyes I can see absolutely nothing. Only imagination sees him leaning to speak through the crack of the closing door, as three words reach me, softly, with a sound of blood-curdling intimacy.

'Touch your ears.'

The man is no longer there. He no longer matters. What matters now is the star, which is there, outside the window, glittering through black leaves, black branches, in the black sky. The star is omnipresent and omnipotent. I feel its radiations at work in me, consuming and disintegrating my humanity. The star can mutate the human element in some way.

The human being I once was I am now no longer. I don't know what I'm supposed to be any more. Things keep changing here, getting lost in the dark. It's very disturbing.

Whatever I am, I'm among the lost things—I do know that.

The Zebra-Struck

M couldn't read the name scrawled on the hospital chart, but saw that it began with the letter K. And K was what he always called her, until the end.

Perhaps she was vaguely aware of a blurred figure, wearing a white coat unfastened and trailing, bent over the chart. Perhaps not. Consciousness came and went in slow tides, unrelated to any particular moment. He looked at her out of his deep-seeing eyes, saw her lips move, bent lower, and heard: '. . . the fourth time. . . .'

It made no sense. But her hair was a brightness in the dull ward; it pleased him, and for a second he was reminded of a fair girl on a bridge . . . somewhere . . . swallows wheeling . . . a long time ago. . . . So that he smiled at her, gave her a friendly and knowing wink, knowing it would be forgotten later. 'Rest now,' he said. 'Don't try to talk.'

But still she persisted, with what infinite labour he could well imagine, dredging up words one by one, with long spaces between them, from the black rising quicksands. 'This is . . . the fourth time . . . I've died. . . .' It took her all day to complete the sentence, and then exhaustion submerged her, her lips were sewn up.

What she had said aroused his interest. It was unexpected. Like a quick-growing plant, something new had sprung up in the dull, repetitious monotone of hospital life. But she had gone now, it was useless to stay any longer. He walked away down the long ward without looking round, knowing he would come back to the bed tomorrow.

Just for a moment she had revived the lost years, the lost youth. He fitted her face and bright hair into the past as if she belonged there; as if she had known his lost self, the poet who was forgotten.

For him that was how it started.

She had told him only the truth. There had been no exhibitionism, no acting, in those other deaths. Each time she'd been so certain it was the last that, beyond the horrid physical details—dissolving capsules, choking, nausea, painful injections—had been the terror of annihilation, the screaming protest of the creative impulse she was assassinating with brutal violence, despite its determination to survive.

The four failures had been anything but deliberate. Accidents, of taking too much or too little, of being found too soon.

Each time the horror of returning consciousness had made it impossible ever to try again. Except that the other horror was so much greater. Life, which had at no time been kind or easy, always retracting, imprisoning her in smaller and smaller cells, where she was for ever cut off from laughter, love and adventure and all she valued.

Now there was no future for her, no more left. Nothing was left but the fifth and last death . . . it must be conclusive . . . it had to be died in desperate determination . . . . The fifth time she must escape, before the ultimate horror of walls closing in deprived her of herself, crushed out of all semblance of the human being. . . .

Then M spoke kindly to her in the gloomy ward, and everything changed. Lying there waiting for him, wondering if he would come, if he really existed or she had invented him, she felt the future collecting for her, preparing. . . .

It has something to do with the cosmic rays coming from outer space. They strike some person or thing, and then you get a mutation—like the stripes on a zebra.

The attraction of two such mutants to one another would have an almost incestuous appeal and be far stronger than the bond of love between ordinary human beings.

Their relationship had not been clearly defined. It had seemed to achieve itself spontaneously, without effort on either side, and with no preliminary doubts or misunderstandings. To her it was both inevitable and invested with dreamlike wonder that, among all the earth's teeming millions, she should have met the one being complementary to herself. It was as if she'd always been lost and living in chaos, until this man had appeared like a magician and put everything right. The few brief flashes of happiness she had known before had always been against a permanent background of black isolation, a terrifying utter loneliness, the metaphysical horror of which she'd never been able to convey to any lover or psychiatrist. Now suddenly, miraculously, that terror had gone; she was no longer alone, and could only respond with boundless devotion to the miracle worker.

He was twelve years older than she and looked older, and as she looked less than her age, they were sometimes taken, much to his amusement, for father and daughter. Her own father had died while she was a child, she couldn't remember him, and she had perhaps always been looking for a substitute father. Well-suited to this role, the man seemed appropriately her superior, with his benevolence, knowledge and academic degrees; his reputation, his poetry, his experience of the world; his successes, catastrophes and adventures. He was very often gay, and often indulged in fantastic imaginings; but also he often seemed to be evolving strange and significant thoughts behind his vast forehead.

Knowing she had his full support and approval, she at last felt safe and happy. For the first time in her life she was appreciated at her true value and began to lose her inferiority feeling and fear of failure. He often praised her, saying she had a quality of timeless beauty in addition to a high degree of intelligence, and was the only woman whose thoughts always kept pace with his—were sometimes even a jump ahead. She was fascinated by the idea of this secret affinity, though how it was supposed to have come about was not fully explained. She understood only that a mutation accounted for their instantaneous mutual attraction, as it did for her former terrible loneliness, and that cosmic rays were responsible, in the same way that they were for the zebra's stripes. But he never made clear, and she could never be certain, whether this esoteric theory was meant to be taken seriously, or was one of the many complicated games he played in his head.

On the whole she was inclined to believe in the cosmic rays, if only because, apart from them, they had so little in common to explain their wonderful understanding:

nationality, upbringing, character, were all different. More-
over, the man was an exceedingly complex, uncompromis-
ing, intransigent individualist, subject to unpredictable
moods and impulses hard to comprehend or meet with
equanimity. Yet he wrote a poem beginning :

> Our smiles have bridged the gulf
> where shadow grows under the lightless day. . . .

and it was perfectly true that their smiling glances had
crossed an abyss each of them had believed impassable.

She was delighted to be included in his mysterious games,
admitted to his world of imagination which no one else
had been allowed to enter. As she gained confidence
under his influence, he encouraged her to take an active
part in the fantasies he invented, with which her elabora-
tions merged indistinguishably, so that they seemed part
of the original concept. She herself was surprised by the
closeness of their collaboration and the intimate interplay
of their inventiveness, almost as if her brain had access to
his.

It was the cosmic rays, he said, that made this degree
of empathy possible, uniting them much more closely than
normal lovers, so that communication between them was
on the level future generations would attain through their
greatly heightened sensibilities.

He seemed to speak quite seriously and simply of their
privilege in thus being able to sample the experience of
those happy inhabitants of a future world. But often when
discussing such topics he became metaphysical and obscure,
making use of unfamiliar terminology and symbols which
confused and mystified her. She couldn't entirely suppress
a suspicion that he mystified her deliberately, which was

disturbing because it suggested a fundamental elusiveness in him.

Quite often he introduced new inventions, presenting them as alternative versions of truth, as if he was determined not to reveal himself fully, even to her. But as nothing else about him gave this impression, it was easy for her to forget it, and most of the time she did. He had said he wanted to give her the love and security that had been missing from her childhood, and to depend on him in childlike trusting devotion was her idea of heaven. Doing so, at last she could relax in blissful contentment. It was enough for her to be with him for everything to seem straightforward, simple and safe. Forgetting all the storms and stresses, the ceaseless anxiety and appalling isolation she had known in the past, she floated in complete serenity, not even conscious, for long periods, of the suspicion which constituted the one flaw in her happiness.

If she did think of it, she dismissed the thought instantly. He was the kindest, most reliable, most conscientious of men; it was monstrous to suppose he could be in any way irresponsible. Yet always, after a long interval, she would again catch sight of something indefinably evasive in him; something so irreconcilable with the rest of his character that, besides threatening her tranquil dependent state, the discrepancy was disquieting in itself. Such glimpses, however, were too few and far between to disturb her seriously. She saw that she must never impinge on him by becoming over-assertive, and kept herself to some extent in the background, so that their arguments remained unheated and friendly, although they discussed all their ideas with endless enthusiasm. Since neither of them had money, there was not much else they could do,

But both were content to wander about for hours through the streets and parks, talking interminably about whatever came into their heads.

When she first went to his house after leaving the hospital she was frightened. She was still not quite stabilized, the margins of reality were not yet distinctly marked, she was afraid she might have imagined his sympathetic attitude and would now confront someone quite different—someone wearing the usual mask-face of non-interest and uncomprehending indifference, which meant that no communication was possible. She entered the house, and was taken without delay straight to an upper room, where he immediately came forward, smiling and giving her both his hands. In a flash all her apprehensions had vanished, she knew instantly that everything was all right, he was real, not an image she had invented to suit her needs. The relief was so tremendous that she was out of herself for a second, floating in sheer happiness, and was surprised the next moment to find she'd sat down in a chair.

'Relax!' he was saying. 'Why are you so anxious? Don't you trust me? You'll see, I shall put you in cotton wool.'

How heavenly it had been then to feel her old lonely fears dissolving as she sank into the soft, warm, blissful security he wrapped round her; a miracle for which she would be eternally grateful.

In his quiet, intimate, humorous voice he had told her : 'You mustn't be so afraid of life—it's all we've got. Don't let it hurt you so much.'

Their eyes met for a moment. And the glance that flickered between them had been a wordless message of understanding, the affirmation of a sympathetic secret alliance from which everyone else was excluded by natural law—the close mysterious blood-bond between two mutants, of which she had not yet heard. But, in some indescribable fashion, it had seemed, even then, that, obscurely, everything was already known and had been accepted, accepted finally and absolutely, in the depths of her unconscious self.

'Take off your scarf,' he had said presently.

Surprised, she obeyed, only realizing when she was holding it that for once she had not been painfully reminded of circumstances associated with the mustard coloured silk splashed with black and crimson, which had been given to her when a precarious marriage was collapsing in sordid ruins.

The man got up from his desk and came to stand directly in front of her, gazing down at her silently until she began to be faintly embarrassed by his intent regard. He had a strange, irregular, deeply-lined face, extremely flexible and expressive, which at the moment seemed lit from inside by sympathy and intelligence. Suddenly he leaned towards her, and the next moment she felt his hands on her forehead, which was high and bulged slightly and childishly in a way she disliked and tried to conceal by covering it with her hair. With incredibly gentle movements, his strong, firm hands were moving the fringe aside, caressing her forehead with slow, soothing, hypnotic strokes, and finally shaping themselves to her head as if holding a fragile cup. All her self-consciousness had been smoothed away, she felt happy, and peaceful, wanting nothing except to stay as she was, steeped in complete serenity.

'Why do you hide your forehead?' he asked very softly, not wanting his voice to disturb the trance his hands had induced. 'Your forehead is beautiful and I love it. One day I'll write a poem about it. It expresses so much of you : your childhood, your travels, your love affairs; all the things that have formed your essential self.'

There was no need for her to answer or move. Relaxed and happy, she listened as to a dream-voice speaking, utterly peaceful, convinced that whatever happened must be for the best. Everything that had troubled her had been left far behind. At last she had found the right place, the place she most wanted, alone with the man who could perform this miracle. He was still bending over her, keeping his hands on her head, which seemed perfectly right and proper.

At length the slight pressure came to an end, he stepped back, and she experienced a momentary disappointment, but hardly had time to register the feeling before, with a sudden change of mood, he said :

'Come into the other room. I want to show you my pictures.'

His voice was cheerful and matter of fact, an unexpected, young, smiling look that was almost mischievous came on his face as he led her across the landing, taking her arm. She had not realized then that she was about to undergo a sort of test, that he judged people by their reaction to these paintings; only later was she thankful that her stammered remarks appeared to have satisfied him. At the moment of entering the room opposite, which was dominated by three extraordinary pictures, she was quite unaware of anything but the impact of the pictures themselves.

She had never seen paint so amazingly brilliant, or used quite in this way, or with such an overpowering sense of drama or tragedy, which was all the more striking because the vivid colours were those normally associated with gaiety. Cerise, and sharp pinks and vermilions were in violent clashing contrast with startling yellow and orange, black, cerulean and Prussian blue, acid greens and a virulent vibrant purple, splashing the walls, on this dull day, like fierce tropical sunshine.

As she began to recover from the onslaught of sheer colour, she saw that one picture was of a group of semi-stylized nudes, the figures repeating the shapes and hues of massive violet-shadowed volcanic rocks in an indigo sea. Its effect would have been lively and stimulating but for the sinister undertone, which was much more marked in the other two paintings. One of these was unmistakably a portrait of the man, painted ten or fifteen years earlier, when he was about thirty, seated beside what looked like a feminine counterpart of himself, pared down to the skeleton, with a greenish, transparent, distraught face and extraordinary weeping eyes, liquidized in their sockets, reminding her of a description of the effects of Napalm— 'their eyes melted and ran down their cheeks'. The incandescent colours intensified the ominous, weird element to the pitch of horror, and she turned quickly to the third painting, which was slightly more subdued in tone. This was another portrait, of a melancholy, neurotic looking woman, who was gazing over her shoulder with a profoundly disturbing, haunted expression.

Glancing at her companion, she saw with a shock that his expression was almost identical with that of the woman's painted face, and a tremor of apprehension went through her. His reassuring smile reappeared immediately. But she couldn't forget the other solitary, elusive, impenetrable look, which defied definition. Later on, when she knew it better, she decided that its alarming quality was its remoteness, as if his gaze came from somewhere so immeasurably far off that she couldn't even be sure it was meant for her, and not for someone he'd known in another country, at a different stage of existence.

During the weeks and months that followed, she occasionally caught sight of this peculiar look, always feeling the same small shiver, which she at once suppressed, refusing to investigate or even acknowledge it. Nothing could really disturb her at this time, or penetrate the bliss which surrounded her like a cocoon. In the benign atmosphere of his encouragement and affection, she felt herself growing more assured and intelligent every day, until it seemed as if she was a real member of the zebra elite, and that she could understand anything, however abstruse, as long as they were together. There was no end to what they had to say to each other. But although they discussed every topic under the sun in the course of their roaming through parks and side streets, the talk never became solemn, but was always full of the gay surprises of two hitherto solitary minds suddenly discovering communication.

Another poem of his which started :

> Through all the rain and restlessness of snow
> We went together in the shadow year. . . .

later contained the lines :

> We walked together secret and unswerving
> through all the ways of light and shadowed streets,
> unheeding as the wind. . . .

Years later, the words could recall the happiness of being isolated with him, in a world apart, both of them walking anonymous and as if invisible, the whole sky, streets and buildings were invested with a sort of wild unearthly splendour that was all theirs, and was theirs alone. Shared with him, the isolation she used to dread produced this near-ecstatic sensation. They were immeasurably removed from the passers-by, whose indifference pinned them together more closely, isolating them in their unique loneliness, apart from all other beings.

They never felt any need for people. Exchanging glances before others, a secret understanding would flash between them, sign of an intimacy no one else could share. They only wanted to be alone together, the presence of outsiders was merely an intrusion, a check on the freedom of communication existing between them in solitude. How could they not resent having to waste their precious time talking to strangers? She, especially, couldn't bear anyone else to be with them, not even someone she'd known for years, and would work herself into a frenzy of suppressed impatience until she'd succeeded in getting rid of the superfluous individual boring them with futile gossip and commonplaces. In this way she gradually lost touch with most of the people she'd known, who not unnaturally felt affronted by her behaviour.

On one occasion when her telephone rang while they were together, the man was struck by her hasty, off-hand, distracted replies and evident anxiety to finish the conversation, so that he asked why she was neglecting her old friends and the life she used to lead with them.

'Friends? Life?' she repeated with real surprise. 'I have no life except with you. And no friends either. They've just faded out.'

'You could soon make them reappear.'

She gazed at him with a slight uncomprehending frown. 'Why should I, when I don't want anybody but you?'

'Why not? Can't you tell me?' His voice was quiet and absolutely composed. Only his face, most curiously, had begun to shine with a secret triumph too strong to hide—the over-riding triumph of victory.

Feeling suddenly inarticulate, she did not see, did not look at him, but said at last: 'Because I only feel truly alive when I'm alone with you.'

'Splendid!' As if to conceal his triumph he burst out laughing. 'And you really don't want other people? You don't miss your old life?' Now the strong triumphant note was loud in his voice, and it caught her attention.

'What questions!' she exclaimed, smiling. 'You must know you're the only person who's ever made me feel at home in the world. I couldn't have any existence apart from you.' She continued to smile at him, unprepared for the intensity of his next words.

'How glad I am that I found you! You must stay with me always—to the very end.'

He was looking at her with the greatest affection, there seemed no cause for the sudden cold fear that now made her say, in an uncertain voice she hardly meant him to hear, 'And what about after that?'

He did hear, however, and answered firmly, 'There's no need to worry about afterwards.'

Later, when she tried to recall how he'd looked when he said it, his expression eluded her. But at the time she had been satisfied.

They made no regular arrangements about meeting. When he was especially busy and absorbed in his work, he sometimes stayed away for days. It frequently happened

then that, just when she felt she couldn't go on any longer
without him, they would meet by chance, in the street,
or at somebody's house, and the relationship which had
been in abeyance would instantly be renewed with fresh
ardour.

At the same time, she couldn't help becoming more
aware of that elusiveness in him which she found so
frightening. He was everything she wished him to be,
loving, loyal, protective. Yet, every now and then, he
would glide away, leaving her vulnerable and insecure,
pierced by agonizing doubts. Her secret fear was that, in
some way too terrifying to put into words, he would finally
elude her altogether.

At night when she couldn't sleep, the strange paintings
would haunt her, horrific under their primitive, violent,
gay colours, particularly the woman's neurotic face with its
ghastly resemblance to his. It was terrible to see his eyes
looking out of that same inaccessible solitude—not to know
whether he even saw her.

Even when he looked at her with his normal friendli-
ness, she couldn't forget the dismaying glimpse of a distance between them which she'd never be able either to
cross or abolish. If only she could be certain that his
intimate expression was meant for her! But there was no
way of knowing : it was not a question that could be asked.
She was always afraid he might be looking through her
at someone known long ago, in quite different circumstances.

She wondered about these strangers she would never
meet, now dead or scattered around the world, who to
him were still so alive and present. He often talked about
them, especially about the painter of the impressive pictures, to whom he had been closely attached, and who

still seemed to exert some influence over him, even from beyond the grave. Without being exactly jealous of him, she found it painful that he should have something she could never share. Ashamed, she ordered herself to be satisfied with what she had, their wonderful friendship, the understanding that never failed or diminished with the passing years. For her, the man was the whole of life, not merely its centre; and she knew this was not, and never had been, true of him in relation to her, which was painful.

Her fear of losing him became more conscious and more insistent, as more and more often he seemed to withdraw to a place where she couldn't follow, looking out with grey, solitary, unreadable eyes. She could never be sure now, even at their moments of greatest intimacy, that he wouldn't abandon her suddenly. He would abruptly announce, 'I must go home and work,' then jump up, barely remembering to say goodbye before he hurried out of the flat. From the window she watched him striding away from her, an isolated, mysterious, nocturnal prowler, moving as swiftly and silently as a cat, and with the same air of stealthy detachment from everything, intent on his own private concerns, in a different world, millions of miles away. He never looked round. And with this painful impression of alienation she would be left until she saw him again.

Telephoning after one such occasion, he told her to expect him that evening, and promised to be with her by ten o'clock. She was in a mood of acute disequilibrium, which nothing could put right but his reassuring presence, for which she'd been longing all day. The wait till ten seemed interminable, and when there was no sign of him then she steeled herself to wait again, repressing anxiety, keeping occupied, trying not to look at her watch all the time. But, as the long minutes crawled past, and further great unendurable tracts of waiting loomed up before her, intolerable as vast empty deserts to a sufferer from agoraphobia, she gradually grew almost frantic. By twelve she was convinced he wasn't coming at all.

When, not long after midnight, he arrived, and was apparently astonished by her distress, she couldn't stop herself asking why he was so late—had he forgotten he'd promised to come at ten?

'No, I didn't forget, but I had to finish something,' he said, as if no apology or further explanation were needed.

'But after you'd promised—why didn't you ring up and say you'd be late?' She broke the resolution she'd kept for years by letting her voice sound reproachful. But he merely looked blankly at her, as if she'd said something completely unreasonable.

'I was working. How could I ring up?'

She saw the futility of going on, even while her lips involuntarily reshaped the words : 'But you promised. . . .'

Unshakeable, uncomprehending, he repeated, 'I was working,' with a touch of exasperation this time, so that she said no more, and for a hateful moment felt she knew nothing whatever about him.

It was very strange. He had such understanding of everything about her. How could he not know when he frightened and hurt her? He gave so much and so generously, supporting her absolutely, unfailingly—until the moment when, all at once, he was no longer there. She never knew when it would happen. They might be walking together in the streets round his home, or playing out one of the inexhaustible episodes of their

E

serial games, or discussing whatever it was among the spinning galaxies or the grains of dust. Suddenly, without warning, the enclosed magic circle of their intimacy would be shattered by an indifferent, distant glance of cold cruel remoteness. She couldn't bear it, and wanted to call him back, to remind him of the cosmic rays that were supposed to have joined them in indestructible closeness—how could he desert her? But, determined not to intrude on his privacy, she kept silent, driving the fear she couldn't eradicate into the deepest recesses of her being.

Deliberate unkindness in him was unthinkable; so she reached the conclusion that, in his creative capacity, he was ruthless without knowing it, from some basic necessity. By degree, she had given up trying to understand. He was too complex for her. She couldn't unravel the many contradictions in him, simply accepting them, as she accepted the fact that she was seeing less and less of him.

The twelve years difference in their ages had now become an enemy and an obstacle to their meeting. He suffered a heart attack and was often ill, withdrawing from her at these times, either out of pride, or in order not to damage the image on which she depended. Seeing him only when he was at his best, she hardly realized the gravity of his condition, was hardly aware of gradual changes in him, and felt slightly aggrieved when he shut himself up at home and declined to see her. However, he had only to reappear for her grievance to be forgotten and everything to be just as it always had been.

At once the old magic revived, uniting them in their supra-normal alliance.

After one of his illnesses, when she hadn't seen him

for several weeks, she became ill herself, as if from the deprivation of his company. She was feverish, and felt an almost irresistible longing for him; their last meeting seemed incredibly distant, as if it had taken place in another age altogether. Hour by hour, her obsession grew stronger and she more disturbed—she must, must, see him, even if only for a few minutes. She controlled herself to a point during the day, but as her temperature rose towards evening, she so far abandoned her ingrained consideration as to telephone and ask him to come and see her. An unknown voice answered, saying that he was not yet well enough to go out; which he must have overheard, for he snatched the receiver, and in a tone unfamiliar to her promised to come quite shortly.

To hear him speak in that strange voice, sounding both strained and upset, increased her nervous distress. Perhaps he really was too unwell to come, she wondered guiltily whether to ring again and tell him it was unnecessary; but after a few undecided moments, her craving for his presence obliterated these doubts.

The fever mounting in her as she waited, she swung uneasily between nightmarish half-dreams and the scarcely more reassuring reality of her lonely flat, where he was the only visitor. Too restless to stay in bed, she wandered about aimlessly between spells of watching for him from the window, hardly able to contain her longing for his arrival to rescue her from the hallucinatory fever world—he himself seemed one of its frightening illusions when she saw him lurching and stumbling towards her door, his bare domed head white under the street lights.

The sight of this pathetic, unsteady figure, instead of the swift catlike prowler she was expecting, came to her as a violent, agonizing, astounding shock. It was as if she had worn his image like a locket in her heart ever since their first meeting, and only now, this moment, saw how much he had altered since then. He looked so fragile and ravaged by illness that she was horrified and for the first few seconds only wanted to take him to some safe quiet place where he could rest and recover and she could make him smile.

But when he entered the room she suddenly saw, through the mists of fever, that his elusiveness had assumed a new and terrible form. Panic engulfed her, sweeping away restraint, and she clutched his hand, gazing speechlessly at him, her eyes filling with tears. Suddenly she'd remembered the anguish of irremediable loneliness to which she had once been condemned, but which she'd believed she had escaped for ever. All at once, it was threatening her again, obscuring everything else. Without knowing it, she let him lead her back to bed, but would neither lie down nor let go of his hand, distracted by semi-delirious fear and the threat of her old metaphysical dread, and further confused and confounded by her own incredible blindness.

'Don't leave me!' she cried in acute distress and confusion, clinging to him as though she was drowning.

'Of course I won't leave you.' The man spoke and smiled with careful kindness, calling upon the principles of a lifetime to help him deal with the situation, although it was evident that he was far too frail and depleted to do so.

She saw the pathos of his ageing face, which was now that of his counterpart in the portrait, without the colour, but with the same haunted transparent look, the same sad, sick, almost melting eyes. But still her irrational fear remained stronger than any other emotion; she was desperate

for his assurance that he would not abandon her in the
terrifying way now in the process of being made clear
to her.

'Don't leave me alone. Don't go away. Promise you'll
stay with me.'

'I promise,' he said, gently disengaging himself from
her clutching hand. 'Try to be quiet. It's no good suffering
like this. I won't let you suffer.'

He was frowning as he turned to open his briefcase,
which he had put on a chair. A moment later, she saw
from his expression that he'd ceased to see her, and was
seized by wild agitation. All the time he was preparing an
injection, she went on pleading with him, beseeching and
begging him not to betray her, not to slip away, not to
leave her alone in a hostile world where she didn't belong, her tear-choked, frantic, fever-voice speaking wildly
of mutants and cosmic rays and their unbreakable
union.

He didn't hear her. He was not listening. He had re-
treated into himself, the absent look on his face a pro-
tection against a too painful, too difficult situation, the
demands of which he lacked the strength to fulfil. He left
it to his professional conscience, which deputized for him,
speaking with automatic professional kindliness and reassurance all the time he was going in and out of the bathroom
and delving into his briefcase, keeping up a soothing,
gentle, imperturbable singsong, as if pacifying a child or
a mental patient.

'Now you must sleep,' he said, when he approached the
bed with the filled syringe in his hand.

She had stopped crying and fallen back on the pillow in
dumb despair; and for a moment he stroked her forehead,
and even seemed to see her.

'Don't be frightened. I promise I won't betray you.' With an excellent rendering of an affectionate, comforting smile, he pinched up the skin of her arm and inserted the needle.

She turned her head slightly towards him while the plunger went down. But his eyes were now lowered to watch the syringe, and he didn't look at her again. Already he seemed to have gone far away, and to be receding further and further each second into the frightful new strangeness which terrified her beyond words, now that at last she was starting to understand it.

Rousing herself to a last frenzied spasm of effort, she tried to will his attention to her. 'Come back! I can't live without you! Have you forgotten the zebras? You can't desert me. . . . You said yourself we must stay together until the end . . . you told me not to worry about afterwards. . . .' But the words that should have streamed out of her mouth in agonized screams came forth, if at all, as faint whispers.

He seemed unaware, withdrawing the needle, pressing cotton wool on the arm, with his remote, automatic efficiency.

'He's gone. I'm alone again,' she thought, in an extremity of despair, hopelessness washing over her like the sea.

But, as if to disprove the thought, he evoked the ghost of benign paternal authority and compassion. 'Sleep, poor lost lonely child. I promised you shouldn't suffer, and you see I'm keeping my promise. I always do.'

He had smiled down at her as he finished speaking, a charming, gentle, half-mournful smile. While his inscrutable, deep-sunk, liquescent eyes gazed out from an absolute solitude so totally inaccessible that she was hunted

by it through her racing unlucky dreams all night long;
and would be hunted through all the nights of her life
afterwards.

A Town Garden

I know people envy my town garden. They feel indignant because I have a garden all to myself, right in the city centre, where there's such a shortage of space.

Here are we, they say, stuck in flats miles up in the air, or else underground and so dark we must keep the lights on all day, packed as close to our neighbours as goods on the shelves of a supermarket, not a tree or a blade of grass visible anywhere, nothing but walls and traffic. Our feet are always standing on concrete floors, or pounding on life-less pavements, we hardly know whether we're indoors or out. Lifts swoop down with our children from the heights of concrete tower blocks to playgrounds in concrete yards. On every side we are surrounded exclusively by things that are hard, huge, hideous, made by man. If, at the week-end, longing for a glimpse of the natural world, we make the tiring, tedious journey to one of the public parks, it's always a great disappointment. The same craving will have driven there countless others, who will be swarming all over it so that we can't even see the grass. There is no grass, as a matter of fact: whenever a small patch of ground does appear, it turns out to consist of bare earth, from which the grass has been worn by innumerable tramping feet. All the grass we ever see is an occasional

136

brown, withered, dried-up tuft. The dusty trees look
dejected, deformed, degraded, their lower branches smashed
by hooligans, their bark disfigured by hacked obscenities.
The leaves come out reluctantly, late in the season, and
at once start to shrivel and turn yellow, poisoned by smoke
and fumes, too discouraged to live in the city for more
than a day.

There's nothing to sit on but a few dilapidated old
chairs which are practically falling apart and often
collapse under you. And even these are so scarce and so
much in demand that anybody who gets one is instantly
surrounded by predatory prowlers determined to snatch it
away. Day after day, these broken-down chairs get more
and more damaged in successive disputes. Peace and quiet
aren't to be thought of with so many noisy arguments going
on, besides the noise made by children, dogs and transis-
tors. Gangs of teenagers add to the uproar, pushing through
the crowd, creating disturbances and confusion, uttering
sudden loud unexpected yells, frightening old people and
knocking down children, as aggressive and impudent as
packs of wild dogs.

These aren't the only drawbacks to the parks either.
People in the mass are unprepossessing, particularly in
hot weather. In summer they go about almost naked,
great fat women displaying their mountainous buttocks
and dangling breasts without the slightest restraint. The
men, fiddling about with their crotches, are just as un-
appetizing; bandy, knock-kneed; their limbs shrivelled
flabby appendages, or else muscle-bound monstrosities;
chests grub-white or matted with sweat-sodden curls; smelly
fungus sprouting in every axilla. On a thundery day, the
stink of all these exposed sweaty bodies is nauseating and
hangs over the whole park, stronger than the fumes of

diesel oil from the nearby traffic. It's unbearable, one starts coughing and choking and holding one's breath, trying not to inhale it. But as human beings must breathe, the only thing to do is to leave as quickly as possible. We've worn ourselves out for nothing.

Bad tempered, disgruntled, with aching feet, we start the long journey back, our peevish children lagging behind, their clothes stained and crumpled, their puny mewling faces unrecognizable under a tear-streaked coating of dirt and chocolate. We're too fed-up and exhausted to care whether these miserable grizzling kids trailing after us are our own or somebody else's; we only want to get home and rest. Our spirits are weighed down by disgust and frustration; while, on the physical plane, our arms are almost dragged out of their sockets by the deadweight of all the stuff we brought with us—paint-boxes, cameras, picnic-baskets; heaven knows what ridiculous relics of ancient hopes, again disappointed.

Yes, I see how unfair it must seem for me to have my own garden, right in the midst of those same walls and streets which prevent them from seeing a single leaf. They stare silently as I pass on the pavement, then huddle together and mutter among themselves, gazing after me with vindictive faces. 'That's her. That's the one with the garden,' they whisper behind my back. 'I bet some crookery went on there.' 'She looks a shady character.' 'Looks up the pole.' 'Always alone, never see her with anyone else— that's a bad sign.' 'Not normal.' 'Shows something's wrong.' 'I always said so.'

Yes, I suppose people are bound to feel resentful and to dislike me. But they shouldn't jump to conclusions about my garden. I wonder how many of them would change places with me if they knew what it's really like here.

When they go home and open the door they must be surrounded immediately by children and relatives, whose voices follow them everywhere, laughing, chattering, asking questions. Things are very different in this garden. No voice ever speaks, I'm completely alone here and always will be, cut off from the rest of the world.

The day is warm, grey and quiet. I sit on the bench from which nearly all the paint has peeled off. My garden is the size of a largish room, and seems enclosed like a room, on account of the walls all round it. It's like a room that's been empty so long everyone has forgotten about its existence. The wall behind the bench is the wall of my house. On the left is the grey, windowless wall of the house next door, on which an old dying vine has traced the obscure calligraphy of its twisted stems. Ten-foot brick walls, trees and bushes are on the other two sides. Overshadowed like this the garden gets little sun, and today there's no sun at all, and therefore no shadow. Although the earth and the stones are quite dry, my impression is of a dark, damp room, full of deep shade, as it might be full of water. There isn't a breath of wind. Nothing moves. Not a living creature is to be seen; not a flower either. The plants are straggling and overgrown, the strongest choking those that are more delicate.

Suddenly now it seems that this silent secluded garden is really less like a room than an excavation, it could be a cellar, a dungeon, some sunken place. Suddenly I feel I'm a prisoner here; walls all round and the low grey lid of the sky overhead. The trees are so still. . . . There's something unnatural about the motionless branches. Such stillness. . . . It's almost frightening. It's more like emptiness, nothingness. . . .

I'm shut into this stillness, this lonely silence, without

even a shadow to keep me company. The dusty green leaves hang down as still as if they'd been cut out of metal. Not one of them stirs when the familiar ghost comes drifting towards me through the unmoving trees. Why shouldn't a human being who lives with special intensity imprint himself on places he frequents, and be visible later to someone on the right wave-length? Now he passes quickly, not looking at me, putting his toes down before his heels, as if testing the solidity of the earth he has long ceased to walk on.

Perhaps I'll be able to talk to him. I jump up, take a step forward, smile, say hullo. He's oblivious of me, apparently. It doesn't surprise me; I'm quite used to his odd behaviour. He's always mysterious, like a magician whose inscrutable actions take place on a different plane. He's just picked up a pointed stick, and is holding it in his hand while he inspects the ground as if searching for something among the plants. He used to like those plants, which weren't always unhealthy, untidy. I don't want him to think I neglect them. But nor do I want to force myself on his notice. So, in a very low voice, a sort of aside, I explain, as if to myself, that I've been too tired lately to work in the garden. Besides, since nobody ever sees it, it doesn't seem worth the trouble. He ignores this. He concentrates on the exact place where he pushes the stick into the earth, and afterwards drops a shiny purple and black kidney shape into the hole, repeating the process again and again, selecting each spot with the same care, as though germination is all that matters, and dependent upon his choice.

Beginning to feel disheartened, I sigh, cough, put my hands in my pockets and take them out, shift my weight from one foot to the other, kick a pebble, stand still again.

Nothing I do makes the slightest difference, he still seems unaware of my presence, doesn't speak, doesn't give me a single glance. 'You might at least look at me just once since you've come here,' I am compelled to say. 'Or did you only come to plant beans?'

Still there's silence, he takes no notice whatever, his attention fixed on the hole he's busily filling with earth, which he pokes into it with the stick. Why can't I get through to him? Must I become a ghost too before we can talk to each other? 'If only you'd taken me with you . . . .' I start saying: then suddenly see that he is no longer there. His enigmatic shadow has left the garden, which once again contains only silence, loneliness and my imprisoned self.

I can't stand it. For a second I think of going out again, doing something, finding someone to talk to. But it's only pretence. I don't move. I know perfectly well that my place is here and that I'll stay here. How still it is. . . . How silent. . . . How lonely. . . .

I sometimes wonder if, in the last resort, the parks with their swarming crowds may not be preferable to the silent emptiness of an enclosed garden, where no one, not even a ghost, ever speaks a word.

Obsessional

It happened between nine and ten in the evening, his usual time. The inner door of the lobby suddenly opened, just as if he'd let himself in with his key, and she turned her head.

The sheer, mad impossibility of his reappearing, now, all these months afterwards, did not check the instantaneous charge of purest joy that went through her like an electric shock. Many miracles had occurred in connection with him, and this could be one more, since cosmic rays and the mystery of mutation had committed them to each other—might they not come together without the body, and not only in dreams?

Already, before her reasoning brain killed the illusion, the words of welcome took shape, her muscles tensed for the suddenly youthful springing up that would take her to meet him, hands outstretched to bring him quickly into the room. 'Oh, I'm so glad you've come. . . .' Already, while in the act of turning, she'd seen his face crumpled in the hunted expression which always struck her as unbearably touching, though she could never decide if it was genuine or assumed, as he said with heart-rending humility—real or false, what did it matter? . . . 'You must not be angry with me because I did not come to see you these last days. I wanted to come—but it has not been possible. . . .'

'Of course I'm not angry,' she would answer. 'All that matters is that you're here now.' And everything would be perfect and understood, any need for explanation, any hint of criticism or sadness past would fade out with his troubled expression, his mouth widening in the warm, amused smile of his usual greeting, in confident anticipation of happiness.

Only of course he was not there this time. The door had opened, but nobody had come in. She got up to shut it, the flying fantasy leaving a black hiatus; in the midst of which she remembered that for once she was not alone, and, feeling the visitor's eyes following her with a question, turned back to him, her own eyes painful from straining to see what had never been visible.

'The wind must somehow have blown it open. Unless a ghost opened it.' She closed the door firmly, with unnecessary force, and returned to the friend; one of the very few who still—out of pity? Curiosity? Force of habit? —spent an occasional evening with her.

He nodded, smiling, with the amiable easy pretence of the unbeliever, tolerant enough to admit to ghosts of his own, before, rather obviously, changing the subject. Conversation continued, sounding unnaturally loud in her quiet room, which seemed to take on an air of pained surprise at the unaccustomed clatter of voices. But it was an effort for her to go on talking, and she soon fell silent, remaining absent, dispirited, more aware of the apparition that had failed to materialize than she was of the living guest, who left early, discouraged by her lack of interest in him, or in anything he could say, and was forgotten almost before he was out of the room.

It was always the same now, the ghost always coming between her and her life in the world, so much more important, since that lost being was still her only companion, and their now-obsolete relationship the one true human contact she would ever have.

The last time she had seen him in the flesh, all the vital force of his life stripped away, his sharpened face had confronted her with such a fearful fixed finality of sightless indifference that she had been frozen in mortal terror, engulfed by abysmal despair. After all the years of unfailing support, his huge, inhuman, deaf, blind inaccessibility was horrifying. He had not kept his promise. He had abandoned her, left her to suffer alone.

Since he'd gone, the world had become unnervingly strange. There was nothing she could do and nowhere she could go. She felt lost, lonely, dazed, deprived of everything, even of her identity, which was not strong enough to survive without his constant encouragement and reassurance. Isolation clamped down on her. For days she saw no one, spoke to no one. The telephone seldom rang. The strangers in the streets seemed frightening, as if they belonged to a different species, pushing, hard-faced, hurrying past her without a glance. Waiting to cross, standing in the middle of the road, traffic tearing in both directions, she had a sense of utter estrangement from the noisy, inconsequential chaos around her, as if she stood in a no–world, peering doubtfully at shadows, wondering if any of them were real.

Despite the frightful blow he'd inflicted on her by the act of ceasing to be, the man who had formerly filled her life was still her only reality. He had gone from the world. She would never see him again. And yet he was always with her, speaking to her, sharing her perceptions; he occupied her completely, leaving no room for life, excluding her from the world. Incapable of living without him, she had made him her ghostly reality. His ghost was better than nothing; it gave her no sense of the supernatural, in which she'd never believed, but at times seemed almost identical with the real man. Even more than while he had been alive, she was obsessed by him in a way that was not altogether pleasant, although, like an addiction, it was essential to her.

He waylaid her everywhere : in avenues with prancing equestrian statues, in tree-lined squares, tube stations, libraries, shops. She knew he was waiting for her in other countries : beside lakes and mountains, in hotels and clinics, at a certain café where all one evening he'd written verses and made drawings for her, under the doomed goggling eyes of the crowded trout in their tank. He naturally frequented the streets and parks where they'd walked so often. Forgotten conversations sprang up and struck her among the tables of restaurants where they'd been together. In the quiet streets of her own district, any half-glimpsed face of a passer-by was likely to startle her with the possibility of being his. She would wake in the morning with the conviction that he was coming to see her, and sit all day watching the door, afraid of missing him if she moved. Or she would suddenly feel him waiting impatiently for her somewhere, and in nightmare anxiety race from one of their old meeting places to another, hours later finding herself at home, exhausted, desolated, almost in tears, not sure whether she'd really been to all those places or only imagined she had.

A flimsy crumpled advertisement she took from the letterbox would, for a split second, become one of his scribbled notes, with an obscene cat drawn in the corner,

the message scrawled in soft purple crayon illegible but for
the words, 'The poor M was here. . . .' She would rush
to the telephone when it rang, expecting, for the first
moment before the voice at the other end spoke in her
ear, to hear his distraught voice utter her name. Almost
daily, in her comings and goings about the town, a distant
figure in a dark blue suit sliced her heart with an imagined
resemblance. Hurrying out one day for a loaf of bread,
suddenly she had a premonition. And, yes, there he was,
walking in the same direction, among the people in front
of her, bending forward slightly as if to thrust his way
through them, hands and arms held a little away from
him—there was no mistaking that characteristic prowling walk. But when she darted forward, eager and smiling,
he became an elderly stranger with a heavy, morose face,
and the ghostly illusion dissolved in the roar and diesel
fumes of a passing bus. She did not wish to escape the
consciousness of him, which nevertheless was a burden,
like a dead body she carried about everywhere and couldn't
bear to relinquish. Going into her workroom, she was half-
surprised not to find him scrutinizing her latest paintings
with a wry, enigmatic smile. Her disappointment darkened
these paintings, already discoloured and splashed by the
boredom and futility of her present existence. All her ac-
tivities had become distasteful, dreary, a weariness to her.
Everything she had ever done had been done for him. Why
should she try to do anything now?

She wandered out restlessly into the darkening garden,
feeling the cool dusk rising round her like water, filling
the small space, already full of his inescapable aura. He
had been in the habit of dropping in for a few minutes
at about this time, roaming round the garden or sitting
there till it got dark. Sometimes, if she'd been specially

preoccupied with her work, she had wished he would
not interrupt her, and this memory caused her a fresh
pang. She never did any work these days, so he could
come whenever he pleased—why wasn't he here now?
As if the thought had invoked it, his hatless, hairless,
dignified skull glimmered transparently for a second against
the leaves at a spot where in other years he had planted
beans. But directly afterwards there was only the deserted
garden where nobody came any more, enclosed like a
dark pool of twilight by trees and high walls, and containing nothing except her sadness and solitude and the
silent watery chill of the rapidly deepening dusk. In the
house, certain parts of the rooms, certain objects, always
vividly evoked his image, and for these she could be
prepared. It was the chance reminders, come upon un-
awares, that stabbed her most cruelly : a coat left on the
settee, simulating his collapsed form sprawled on the green
cushions, taking his pulse with two fingers, motionless with
the fated calm of a man long familiar with the idea that
any moment may be his last.

The haunted vacancy of these darkening ghostly rooms
drove her out into the streets to calm herself by the effort
of walking. But still the relentless seconds assailed her
like arrows one after the other with piercing loneliness,
loss. The lights came on, outlining the shapes of strangers,
whose faces, limbs, voices, gestures, tormented her with
momentary fragments of similarity, which flew away at
a second glance. She even caught sight once, in a dark
entry, of his spectral monocled countenance smiling in-
scrutably as it did from so many snapshots, leaving her
with a famished longing so acute that it seemed physical,
and hardly to be endured. If only, just once more, he
would come in the reassuring solidity she had valued so

lightly while it was accessible to her. She knew exactly how they would meet, his eyes finding hers with absolute certainty, but at once moving on, while his mouth undermined this pretence by breaking into the glad, intimate smile of greeting that always made her forget the other look of pretended indifference—distance—what? What was that element of elusiveness which had been there from the start, confirming itself in the end by his broken promise, like some ancient curse nobody believed in, which had finally come true after all?

The question remained unanswered. Deciding that she was tired enough to go home, she walked, dragging her feet wearily, through the emptying streets, not noticing anything, until arrested by the strong sense of his proximity, a few yards from the house where he'd lived all the time she had known him. Immediately she recalled the last painful occasion she'd been inside it, when his absence had been like a scream in the little rooms, where it was distressingly evident that no one now ever looked at the pictures, or took the books from the shelves. Certain small objects, special favourites he'd often stroked and held in his hands while he talked—a white jade fish, a painted Bengal tiger with a stiff string tail—had been incarcerated behind the glass doors of a cabinet, and glared out mournfully from their prison. She could not bear to see his beloved possessions uncared for, and, as soon as she was left alone for a minute, went out on to the stairs; where something impelled her to put her head round the door of his room, and she had instantly been struck down by most violent grief, as, in the act of reaching out to draw her towards the bed, his soft, strong hands disintegrated in thin air.

It seemed to her now that the door of the garage—the

only place where there was room for his piano—was open
and that he was playing inside; an illusion so powerful
that she moved involuntarily to join him; then, collecting
herself with an effort, walked on in the direction of her
own street. Familiar music he'd often played followed her
as she went, floating after her in the dark; muted, melancholy, incomplete passages that seemed to come from
the middle of some long piece which never ended, the
beginning of which she had never heard. The wistful,
wandering notes affected her with an intolerable sadness.
Nevertheless, at the corner she stopped to listen again; but
now the faint sounds had faded out and she was alone in
the silent and empty darkness.

Walking on, she wondered if it was safe to go to bed,
if she would sleep now. Her legs ached with tiredness as
she climbed the stairs and opened her door. The house
looked dark and desolate inside. She went into the lobby,
putting out one hand to switch off the outside light, and
as she turned her head—never sure which switch controlled
which bulb—to look down the staircase, a ghostly face
glinted into her vision with an expression so heart-break-
ingly apologetic that she almost said aloud, 'Don't look like
that. Nothing matters now that you're here.'

Julia and the Bazooka

Julia is a little girl with long straight hair and big eyes. Julia loved flowers. In the cornfield she has picked an enormous untidy bunch of red poppies which she is holding up so that most of her face is hidden except the eyes. Her eyes look sad because she has just been told to throw the poppies away, not to bring them inside to make a mess dropping their petals all over the house. Some of them have shed their petals already, the front of her dress is quite red. Julia is also a quiet schoolgirl who does not make many friends. Then she is a tall student standing with other students who have passed their final examinations, whose faces are gay and excited, eager to start life in the world. Only Julia's eyes are sad. Although she smiles with the others, she does not share their enthusiasm for living. She feels cut off from people. She is afraid of the world.

Julia is also a young bride in a white dress, holding a sheaf of roses in one hand and in the other a very small flat white satin bag containing a lace-edged handkerchief scented with Arpège and a plastic syringe. Now Julia's eyes are not at all sad. She has one foot on the step of a car, its door held open by a young man with kinky brown hair and a rose in his buttonhole. She is laughing because of something he's said or because he has just squeezed her

arm or because she no longer feels frightened or cut off
now that she has the syringe. A group of indistinct people
in the background look on approvingly as if they are glad
to transfer responsibility for Julia to the young man. Julia
who loves flowers waves to them with her roses as she
drives off with him.

Julia is also dead without any flowers. The doctor sighs
when he looks at her lying there. No one else comes to look
except the official people. The ashes of the tall girl Julia
barely fill the silver cup she won in the tennis tournament.
To improve her game the tennis professional gives her the
syringe. He is a joking kind of man and calls the syringe
a bazooka. Julia calls it that too, the name sounds funny,
it makes her laugh. Of course she knows all the sensational
stories about drug addiction, but the word bazooka makes
nonsense of them, makes the whole drug business seem not
serious. Without the bazooka she might not have won the
cup, which as a container will at last serve a useful purpose. It is Julia's serve that wins the decisive game. Holding
two tennis balls in her left hand, she throws one high in
the air while her right hand flies up over her head, brings
the racket down, wham, and sends the ball skimming over
the opposite court hardly bouncing at all, a service almost
impossible to return. Holding two balls in her hand Julia
also lies in bed beside the young man with kinky hair.
Julia is also lying in wreckage under an army blanket,
and eventually Julia's ashes go into the silver cup.

The undertaker or somebody closes the lid and locks the
cup in a pigeon-hole among thousands of identical pigeon-
holes in a wall at the top of a cliff overlooking the sea.
The winter sea is the colour of pumice, the sky cold as
grey ice, the icy wind charges straight at the wall making
it tremble so that the silver cup in its pigeon-hole shivers

and tinkles faintly. The wind is trying to tear to pieces a few frost-bitten flowers which have not been left for Julia at the foot of the wall. Julia is also driving with her bridegroom in the high mountains through fields of flowers. They stop the car and pick armfuls of daffodils and narcissi. There are no flowers for Julia in the pigeonhole and no bridegroom either.

'This is her syringe, her bazooka she always called it,' the doctor says with a small sad smile. 'It must be twenty years old at least. Look how the measures have been worn away by continuous use.' The battered old plastic syringe is unbreakable, unlike the glass syringes which used to be kept in boiled water in metal boxes and reasonably sterile. This discoloured old syringe has always been left lying about somewhere, accumulating germs and the assorted dirt of wars and cities. All the same, it has not done Julia any great harm. An occasional infection easily cured with penicillin, nothing serious. 'Such dangers are grossly exaggerated.'

Julia and her bazooka travel all over the world. She wants to see everything, every country. The young man with kinky hair is not there, but she is in a car and somebody sits beside her. Julia is a good driver. She drives anything, racing cars, heavy lorries. Her long hair streams out from under the crash helmet as she drives for the racing teams. Today she is lapping only a fraction of a second behind the number one driver when a red-hot bit of his clutch flies off and punctures her nearside tyre, and the car somersaults twice and tears through a wall. Julia steps out of the wreck uninjured and walks away holding her handbag with the syringe inside it. She is laughing. Julia always laughs at danger. Nothing can frighten her while she has the syringe. She has almost forgotten the time when she was afraid. Sometimes she thinks of the kinky-haired man and wonders what he is doing. Then she laughs. There are always plenty of people to bring her flowers and make her feel gay. She hardly remembers how sad and lonely she used to feel before she had the syringe.

Julia likes the doctor as soon as she meets him. He is understanding and kind like the father she has imagined but never known. He does not want to take her syringe away. He says, 'You've used it for years already and you're none the worse. In fact you'd be far worse off without it.' He trusts Julia, he knows she is not irresponsible, she does not increase the dosage too much or experiment with new drugs. It is ridiculous to say all drug addicts are alike, all liars, all vicious, all psychopaths or delinquents just out for kicks. He is sympathetic towards Julia whose personality has been damaged by no love in childhood so that she can't make contact with people or feel at home in the world. In his opinion she is quite right to use the syringe, it is as essential to her as insulin to a diabetic. Without it she could not lead a normal existence, her life would be a shambles, but with its support she is conscientious and energetic, intelligent, friendly. She is most unlike the popular notion of a drug addict. Nobody could call her vicious.

Julia who loves flowers has made a garden on a flat roof in the city, all round her are pots of scarlet geraniums. Throughout the summer she has watered them every day because the pots dry out so fast up here in the sun and wind. Now summer is over, there is frost in the air. The leaves of the plants have turned yellow. Although the flowers have survived up to now the next frost will finish them off. It is wartime, the time of the flying bombs, they come over all the time, there seems to be nothing to stop them. Julia is used to them, she ignores them, she does not look. To save the flowers from the frost she picks them all quickly and takes them indoors. Then it is winter and Julia is on the roof planting bulbs to flower in the spring The flying bombs are still coming over, quite low, just above roofs and chimneys, their chugging noise fills the sky. One after another, they keep coming over, making their monotonous mechanical noise. When the engine cuts out there is a sudden startling silence, suspense, everything suddenly goes unnaturally still. Julia does not look up when the silence comes, but all at once it seems very cold on the roof, and she plants the last bulb in a hurry.

The doctor has gone to consult a top psychiatrist about one of his patients. The psychiatrist is immensely dignified, extremely well-dressed, his voice matches his outer aspect. When the bomb silence starts, his clear grave voice says solemnly, 'I advise you to take cover under that table beside you,' as he himself glides with the utmost dignity under his impressive desk. Julia leaves the roof and steps on to the staircase, which is not there. The stairs have crumbled, the whole house is crumbling, collapsing, the world bursts and burns, while she falls through the dark. The A.R.P. men dig Julia out of the rubble. Red geraniums are spilling down the front of her dress, she has forgotten the time between, and is forgetting more and more every moment. Someone spreads a grey blanket over her, she lies underneath it in her red-stained dress, her bag, with the bazooka inside, safely hooked over one arm. How cold it is in the exploding world. The northern lights burst out in frigid brilliance across the sky. The ice roars and thunders like gunfire. The cold is glacial, a glass dome of cold covers the globe. Icebergs tower high as mountains, furious blizzards swoop at each other like

white wild beasts. All things are turning to ice in the
mortal cold, and the cold has a face which sparkles with
frost. It seems to be a face Julia knows, though she has
forgotten whose face it is.

The undertaker hurriedly shuts himself inside his car,
out of the cruel wind. The parson hurries towards his
house, hatless, thin grey hair blowing about wildly. The
wind snatches a tattered wreath of frost-blackened flowers
and rolls it over the grass, past the undertaker and the
parson, who both pretend not to see. They are not going
to stay out in the cold any longer, it is not their job to
look after the flowers. They do not know that Julia loves
flowers and they do not care. The wreath was not put
there for her, anyhow.

Julia is rushing after the nameless face, running as fast
as if she was playing tennis. But when she comes near she
does not, after all, recognize that glittering death-mask. It
has gone now, there's nothing but arctic glitter, she is a
bride again beside the young man with brown hair. The
lights are blazing, but she shivers a little in her thin dress
because the church is so cold. The dazzling brilliance of
the aurora borealis has burnt right through the roof with
its frigid fire. Snow slants down between the rafters, there
is ice on the altar, snowdrifts in the aisles, the holy water
and the communion wine have been frozen solid. Snow is
Julia's bridal white, icicles are her jewels. The diamond-
sparkling coronet on her head confuses her thoughts. Where
has everyone gone? The bridegroom is dead, or in bed
with some girl or other, and she herself lies under a dirty
blanket with red on her dress.

'Won't somebody help me?' she calls. 'I can't move.'
But no one takes any notice. She is not cold any longer.
Suddenly now she is burning, a fever is burning her up.

Her face is on fire, her dry mouth seems to be full of ashes. She sees the kind doctor coming and tries to call him, but can only whisper, 'Please help me . . .' so faintly that he does not hear. Sighing, he takes off his hat, gazing down at his name printed inside in small gold letters under the leather band. The kinky-haired young man is not in bed with anyone. He is wounded in a sea battle. He falls on the warship's deck, an officer tries to grab him but it's too late, over and over he rolls down the steeply sloping deck to the black bottomless water. The officer looks over the side, holding a lifebelt, but does not throw it down to the injured man; instead, he puts it on himself, and runs to a boat which is being lowered. The doctor comes home from the house of the famous psychiatrist. His head is bent, his eyes lowered, he walks slowly because he feels tired and sad. He does not look up so he never sees Julia waving to him with a bunch of geraniums from the window.

The pigeon-hole wall stands deserted in the cold dusk. The undertaker has driven home. His feet are so cold he can't feel them, these winter funerals are the very devil. He slams the car door, goes inside stamping his feet, and shouts to his wife to bring, double quick, a good strong hot rum with plenty of lemon and sugar, in case he has caught a chill. The wife, who was just going out to a bingo session, grumbles at being delayed, and bangs about in the kitchen. At the vicarage the parson is eating a crumpet for tea, his chair pulled so close to the fire that he is practically in the grate.

It has got quite dark outside, the wall has turned black. As the wind shakes it, the faintest of tinkles comes from the pigeon-hole where all that is left of Julia has been left. Surely there were some red flowers somewhere, Julia would be thinking, if she could still think. Then she would think something amusing, she would remember the bazooka and start to laugh. But nothing is left of Julia really, she is not there. The only occupant of the pigeon-hole is the silver cup, which can't think or laugh or remember. There is no more Julia anywhere. Where she was there is only nothing.